SMOKIN' JUSTICE

So Longarm and Foster were shaking adios near the boarding steps of the baggage car when a six-gun cleared its throat for attention, and both lawmen spun away from each other, slapping leather as they went.

Longarm landed in a gunfighter's crouch with his .44-40 trained on a slender dark outline surrounded by thinning gun smoke. But he didn't fire because he could see another figure sprawled on the platform way closer and the tableau only read one way.

"Advance and be recognized, friend," he called.

The mysterious figure who'd just backshot somebody else instead of either lawman moved forward into a puddle of lamplight, a .38 Colt Detective held politely.

"Well, howdy, Henry. I didn't think you had it in you!" said Longarm.

— TABOR EVANS —

LONGARM

AND THE SINS OF SISTER SIMONE

JOVE BOOKS, NEW YORK

This is a work of fiction. Names, characters, places, and incidents are either the product of the author's imagination or are used fictitiously, and any resemblance to actual persons, living or dead, business establishments, events, or locales is entirely coincidental.

LONGARM AND THE SINS OF SISTER SIMONE

A Jove Book / published by arrangement with
the author

PRINTING HISTORY
Jove edition / September 2000

All rights reserved.
Copyright © 2000 by Penguin Putnam Inc.
This book may not be reproduced in whole or in part,
by mimeograph or any other means, without permission.
For information address: The Berkley Publishing Group,
a division of Penguin Putnam Inc.,
375 Hudson Street, New York, New York 10014.

The Penguin Putnam Inc. World Wide Web site address is
http://www.penguinputnam.com

ISBN: 0-515-12910-0

A JOVE BOOK®
Jove Books are published by The Berkley Publishing Group,
a division of Penguin Putnam Inc.,
375 Hudson Street, New York, New York 10014.
JOVE and the "J" design
are trademarks belonging to Penguin Putnam Inc.

PRINTED IN THE UNITED STATES OF AMERICA

10 9 8 7 6 5 4 3 2 1

Chapter 1

It was a balmy spring day in the Rockies. So the columbines were blooming, the grosbeaks were tweeting in the fluttering aspen, and U.S. Deputy Marshal Custis Long of the Denver District Court had an elbow out the window and a three-for-a-nickel cheroot in the grip of his smiling teeth as he enjoyed the morning run of the narrow-gauge Sawtooth Coaster.

Or he did until two elfin heads suddenly appeared above the back of the seat ahead of his to stare wide-eyed and poker-faced at him.

One of the kids wore her corn-silk hair in pigtails. The other was too homely to be anything but a boy. It was the girl who demanded, "You're not really a cowboy, are you? Elmer here thinks you're a cowboy, but I say you have to be a traveling salesman in that brown tweed suit."

Elmer, as her young traveling companion seemed to be named, stuck his tongue out and sneered, "If you're a traveling salesman, how come you're packing a sneaky six-gun cross-draw under that sissy frock coat? If you ain't a cowboy, what are you?"

Longarm, as he was better known in the high country, had been a kid one time. So he took the cheroot from between his teeth to reply in a firm but not unkind tone,

1

"To begin with, I have better manners than some young squirts I could mention. After that, I am neither a cowboy nor a traveling salesman. I am the law, federal, on my way to meet another lawman, Royal Canadian, in Fort Collins. He never told us why."

An older feminine voice rang out from behind Longarm to order the two kids back to their own seats this instant. Neither Elmer nor young Mary Jo, as the pigtailed one seemed to be called, paid their embarrassed-sounding momma or whatever any mind.

Elmer said, "If you're so smart, how come they call this train a *coaster*? I don't see any seacoast around here. We seem to be way high in the Rocky Mountains. So how do you coast in a train when no coast is to be seen to either side of the tracks?"

Longarm decided that was a fair question and explained. "The words of the English language ain't always meant exactly as they might be taken, Elmer. When they accuse a *sailboat* of coasting, they mean it's sailing easy with no effort on the part of its crew, with an offshore or onshore breeze blowing steady across its beam as it follows some coastline or other. When you say you're coasting a *train,* it means the wheels are rolling without much effort down a long gentle grade, with neither the fireman nor brakemen having to do much work, see?"

Elmer said, "No. Why don't they just call it rolling downhill?"

Mary Jo confided, "Elmer has no soul."

Longarm smiled thinly and replied, "I suspected he was lacking in something. But to answer the question, coasting in a boat or aboard a railroad car is sort of in between some effort and a free ride. This line don't run downgrade every mile of the way. Here and there they get to feed the wheels a little steam and, well, I reckon they call this coasting because they think it *feels* like coasting. By the time you kids reach my age, if you manage to live through this stage, you'll have noticed a heap

2

of words don't make much sense if you go over 'em with a fine-tooth comb. I just don't know what *occasional chairs* are when nobody's using 'em as chairs, and I don't care how often a *sitting room* may stand up when nobody's looking. Words mean what they really mean as we *use* 'em, not as we spell 'em, and look at that gray jay out to the east chasing that red-tailed hawk the way a yard dog chases a hobo!"

The two kids fell for it. As they peered out the window at nothing much, the slightly older gal who'd been ordering them back to their own seats swooped past Longarm's left shoulder to grab an ear with either hand and haul them, bawling, into the aisle, where her plan went awry. Mary Jo and Elmer both fell to the floorboards, accusing her of rape or worse as they kicked at her shins above right trim ankles.

So, seeing she was far too young and greenhorned with brats to be their momma, Longarm gallantly rose to grab Elmer by the nape of his neck and the seat of his knee pants, suggesting, "Mary Jo might be a tad easier to drag by both pigtails, ma'am. Where did you say you wanted these two dragged?"

The ash blonde, in a seersucker Dolly Varden dress with her own hair pinned up under a straw boater, was blushing a becoming shade of pink as she flustered, "I do so hope it's true that you're a lawman, good sir. I promised our parents I wouldn't talk to any strange men aboard this train, but a lawman might not count as a stranger when a lady is in difficulty, right?"

Longarm allowed he could fathom her distress if she shared parents with Elmer and Mary Jo. Narrow-gauge railroad cars had regular seats along one side and just the aisle along the other. So as the two more responsible adults herded her little brother and sister back to their own seats, to the considerable amused relief of the few other grown-ups on board, Longarm learned the older sister answered to the name of Willie Mae, but allowed her friends to call her Billie.

As they herded her younger siblings into an end seat, nearest the window, Longarm swung a hardwood seatback forward so he could ride backwards, facing the three of them, as he sternly warned the two kids, "I know you heard your parents tell your elder sister not to hit you. But I am the law, and they never got *me* to promise I wouldn't beat you with a big black whip. So simmer down and enjoy the scenery and the next time the candy butcher comes through I might buy us all some soda pop."

Billie, Billie Butler as it turned out, said it was wrong to bribe children with sweets. He innocently asked what sweets she was talking about, and hoped neither precocious brat would grasp his meaning when he added they'd be coming to the end of the line pretty soon.

He hoped in vain. Little Mary Jo said, "Pooh! You just made that pop up to make us behave, and I'll bet you don't have any big black whip either!"

Longarm snubbed out his cheroot politely as he grudgingly allowed, "Mayhaps not a *big* black whip. But I have a fair-sized riding quirt lashed to my saddle in the baggage car. Do you have someone meeting you all at Juniper Junction, Miss Billie?"

She answered innocently, "Not at the junction itself. We're on our way to a family gathering in Fort Collins."

Elmer said, "Our Aunt Maude is fixing to marry up with an Indian."

Billie laughed weakly and said, "Not an Indian. An Indian agent at the Kimoho Reserve just south of Fort Collins. We'll be able to catch another train there from Juniper Junction, won't we?"

Longarm stared soberly out at the passing scenery and tried to tell himself it was none of his business even as he heard himself telling her, "Not hardly, Miss Billie. They call it a junction because more'n one of these

4

narrow-gauge mountain lines meet there by a river ford and wagon trace east. There's no practical way to run narrow-gauge stock on standard gauge and vice versa, so nobody's tried to down in Juniper Junction. There's a so-called stage line running mud wagons to Fort Collins around three in the afternoon. They let the passengers off all these mountain short lines sort of pile up for the one-a-day run they can make a profit on, see?"

He could see she did, and it was to her credit that she didn't bawl outright. The young gal, who would be stuck with two mulish brats for the better part of a day in a place as tedious as Juniper Junction, just said the three of them would find something to do there until they could get the hell on out.

Longarm tried to keep his mouth shut. But he knew they'd make it to the junction well before noon, and the two kids were already travel-cranky and hard to control. So the next thing he knew he'd said, "I was fixing to hire a saddle mount at the livery in Juniper Junction, Miss Billie. But I reckon I could just as easy charge a one-horse buggy to my traveling expenses. I'm allowed six cents a mile when traveling on official duties, and they just ordered me by wire to get on over to Fort Collins. So, seeing it won't cost near six cents a mile for the four of us to drive in from the junction by livery buggy, what do you say?"

Billie Butler didn't answer as her common sense wrestled with the late Victorian rules of conduct for a proper young lady.

A voice behind Longarm suggested, "Oh, for heaven's sake, take him up on it and I'll be proud to chaperon!"

Longarm turned his head enough to face the older woman seated in a forward riding position with her back naturally close to his own. He ticked his hat brim, smiled uncertainly, and said, "Your servant, ma'am, and you'd be . . ."

"Sloan, the Widow Prunella Sloan, and *my* friends call

me Prune," she demurely replied. As Longarm was taking in her olive complexion, blue-black hair, and smoldering sloe eyes, she added, "I live in Collins and I'd rather be home early than late. So why don't we share the hire of a proper carriage and all ride in together like proper gentry?"

Longarm smiled and turned back to Billie Butler, who shyly decided that as long as Miss Prune would be riding herd on her rep, the notion sure had spitting and whittling half the day in Juniper Junction beat.

So that was how the five of them worked it out, with Longarm getting to wrestle plenty of baggage at the end of the line. He hired an open carriage and team. The ladies got to ride in the back while he drove and the kids sat everywhere, asking if they were almost there yet.

It took a spell, even trotting downhill most of the way. Fort Collins had grown up by a river ford at the north end of the Front Range it shared with Denver. It hadn't been a military fort for some time.

In the days of the beaver trade, some French Canadian mountain man had buried or cached some gunpowder near the crossing and figured that was as good a name as any for the Cache la Poudre River. The army outpost built there in '62 had been swept away in the bodacious floods of '64. But Fort Collins, or Collins as some called it, had lived on as a railroad shipping center and college town. Colorado Agricultural had been founded back in '70 while Colorado was still a territory.

But the downtown Longarm drove into had sprung up well to the northeast of the college campus, around a hub formed by the gathering of College, Linden, and Mountain Avenues, a few blocks from the railroad stop near the site of all that buried gunpowder and the washed-away army outpost.

Before he could settle up at the livery he'd been directed to, he had to drop the others off. He wasn't surprised to see the Butler kids were on their way to a fashionable address closer to the college. As he let them off by a steamboat Gothic mansion, Billie Butler said Longarm was just the sweetest thing and invited him to come calling later if he had a mind to.

As he drove off, with Prunella Sloan perched beside him on the driver's seat now, she chuckled and murmured, "Pretty smooth. From the stories I'd heard about Denver's answer to Don Juan, I'd expected a cruder approach."

Longarm looked pained and replied, "Give me and old Don Juan credit for some common sense, Miss Prune. That maiden-fair we just dropped off can't be more than fifteen or sixteen, soaking wet."

"Eighteen. I asked," said the older and somewhat more maturely built beauty, smoldering darkly in her summer-weight widow's weeds.

When Longarm just clucked at the team, she insisted, "She likes you. A lot. And like me, she's probably heard what they say about you and the fair sex."

Longarm made a wry face and replied, "That's a misnomer for the ways of a maid with a man if ever I heard one, no offense. I would ask you what you'd heard about my wicked ways if I hadn't already heard some of the nonsense my ownself. It ain't true that I once chased Wild Bill out of town or won that shooting contest with Buffalo Bill. I am just a natural man made of mortal clay, Miss Prune. I know you don't want to believe this, because it won't make for much of a conversation with the rest of the gals, but I have been known to hold a door open for a lady or even offer her a ride into town without slobbering all over her like a laughing hyena. Where did you say you wanted me to drop you and that Saratoga trunk off, ma'am?"

She dimpled at him and confessed, "As a matter of fact my place is out beyond that Butler house. But why don't we find out if that lawman from Canada has arrived in Collins yet?"

Longarm thought back, recalled he had told Billie Butler he'd been ordered to meet Crown Sergeant Foster
from Fort MacLeod there in Fort Collins, and conceded,
"His train don't get in till after midnight, and they told
us to meet up in the Burlington House near the depot in
the morning. I don't know why. I reckon Sergeant Foster
will tell me when we get together. You say you live back
the other way, beyond that big Butler place, Miss Prune?"

She said, "Yes. But why don't you turn this rig and
the team in at the town livery first?"

Longarm reined the team to an uncertain walk as he
asked, "How come? That Saratoga in the back is a mite
heavy, no offense, and the livery is over a furlong the
other way."

She said, "Silly. Where do you imagine I left my own
one-horse shay whilst I was visiting our mine in the
mountains? Why don't we do this the sensible way? Turn
this rig in for your deposit and let *me* drop *you* off at
your hotel with that bulky McClellan and Winchester."

So that was the way they worked it, or started to. It
was getting on some by the time Longarm had settled up
at the livery and left the team and carriage for someone
traveling the other way. The hostlers helped him load her
Saratoga and his army saddle aboard her one-horse shay.
As they wheeled out on the avenue, Longarm expected
her to turn towards the Burlington House near the depot.
So he asked where they might be headed when she drove
up a side street to swing along another, which was tiger-
striped by the lengthening shadows of Dutch elm saplings
planted in hopes of more serious shade in the future.

She said that, seeing it was getting on towards supper
time, and seeing he'd refused to let her help pay for that
long carriage ride in from Juniper Junction, the least she
could offer him was a decent home-cooked supper at her
place.

That sounded fair, and it wasn't as if he had anybody
half as pretty waiting for him at a modest small-town

hotel. So he allowed he'd be proud to sup with her, and didn't ask how come they seemed to be sort of sneaking the last block along a cinder-paved alleyway. He knew the carriage houses tended to face back towards such alleyways, and another young widow woman back in Denver didn't seem to want him darkening her front door all that much either, come to study on it.

Chapter 2

As she insisted on helping him stall her horse and store her shay, Prunella Sloan explained how living alone and spending a lot of time out of town on her late husband's far-flung enterprises called for her to retain a once-a-week heavy-cleaning woman and a maid-of-all-work who lived with her own folks and came by as called upon. So there was nobody in the house but her and Longarm as the enterprising widow woman whipped up a simple but tasty supper of venison and fried potatoes, with an offer of canned string beans that Longarm politely but firmly passed on.

They ate at her kitchen table with plenty of Arbuckle brand coffee to go with some mince pie that had set right firm in her pantry while she was away. When she apologized for her pie, he gallantly assured her that, like wine, mince pie improved with age.

Sitting across from him with a calico apron over her weeds and the bodice unbuttoned a bit after working over her stove, Prunella sighed and said, "I wish the same could be said for the rest of us. It seems like yesterday I was a giggly schoolgirl, and here I am, an old widow woman on the sad side of thirty!"

Longarm quietly replied, "We all of us wind up in our

thirties if we don't get our fool selves killed in our twenties, Miss Prune. If you are fishing for compliments, you don't look as old as me and Lord knows you're prettier."

She laughed, said she'd heard he was a sweet-talking man, and told him she was flattered that he'd noticed what she looked like, next to that Butler child. That was what older women called younger gals if they were really worried about them, children. So Longarm offered to wash the dishes. He'd already told the older woman why he'd felt no call to mess with a home gal at a family gathering, for Pete's sake.

The Widow Sloan said to leave the dishes be, lest her maid-of-all-work have nothing to do the next time she dropped by. So they carried their coffee mugs into her front parlor, which was sofly aglow with a fine sunset through her lace curtains. As she waved him to a love seat and sat down beside him, she hesitated, then confessed, "I'd rather not light the lamps in this room, if you don't mind. I suppose I could pull down the shades, but to some nosy neighbors . . ."

"I follow your drift," Longarm soberly replied, as he placed his half-drained mug on the small rosewood coffee table in front of them.

She flustered, "It's not as if it wouldn't be *proper* to entertain a gentleman caller with my poor George a year in the ground before May Day. But to tell you the truth, I've gotten sort of used to living here on my own *without* gentlemen callers, and should word get around that I have commenced to entertain again . . ."

Longarm managed not to frown—it wasn't easy—as he told her, "I just said I followed your drift, Miss Prune. There's this other young widow I know down to Denver who feels much the same about unwelcome callers. I suspect she may be even richer than you, no offense, and hence inclined to question the motives of many a gent bearing flowers, books, or candy. I've assured her more than once that some of them are surely after no more than her fair white body. But she's over thirty too, and so she likely needs as much reassuring."

He resisted the temptation to ask her permission to light up, even though he was dying for a coffee-and-dessert smoke, and added with a thin smile, "It sure beats all how ladies as young as that Miss Billie Butler are convinced we all want to have our wicked ways with their innocent flesh, whilst somewhat . . . more mature young ladies seem just as certain we're only after their money. But that's life, I reckon. We all spend most of it too young or too old to do something or other."

Prunella Sloan sighed and said, "I recall this wall sampler back home in Penn State. It read, 'We get so soon old and so late smart.' I wish I'd understood that better at the time. It's taken me seven years in the Golden West to learn you only get so many grabs at the golden rings before the merry-go-round winds down forever under you!"

Longarm reached for the mug, and drained it this time, before he put it back and asked, "How come we're having such a gloomy conversation with the sunset still smiling through them curtains at us, Miss Prune? I know they make me dress sort of like an undertaker on duty in town these days. But left to my druthers, I'm just a good old boy from West-by-God-Virginia. I hardly ever feel poorly, and I reckon I have a few more grabs at them golden rings ahead of me. So what makes you think you're fixing to kick the bucket before I do?"

She smiled wistfully in the soft gloaming light, and told him that from all she'd heard about him, it seemed a miracle that he was still alive. Then she sighed and said, "But at least you'll be able to say you've *lived* whilst you were alive, once you're dead."

Longarm shook his head and soberly pointed out, "Dead folks don't get to brag all that much, Miss Prune. From the limited conversations I've had with 'em, I suspect hardly any of 'em know they ever lived at all. But

12

you'd best consult your own church elders about such matters, and seeing I seem to depress you so much, I thank you for the swell supper and I reckon I ought to be getting on down the pike."

As he leaned forward to rise, his dark broody hostess placed a firm hand on his thigh and begged him, "Please don't go! The night is young, and didn't you say you didn't expect to meet that other lawman before morning, ah, Custis?"

Longarm leaned back, bemused, to reply, "If he's here by that time. They never offered much detail in that day-rates telegram my home office sent out in the field after me. My boss, Marshal Billy Vail, is disinclined to say more at a nickle a word than he has to. So all I know is that I was told to leave a survey team on their own over in the Shadow Mountain range, and meet Crown Sergeant Foster of the Royal Canadian Mounted Police here in Fort Collins on a matter of international delicacy. That's what they call it when they ain't certain who has jurisdiction, international delicacy."

She murmured that she'd read about him and that last international incident down Mexico way in the *Rocky Mountain News*.

Longarm confided expansively, "I've never had half the trouble with the Mounties as I've had with them Mex *rurales*, even though that El Presidente of theirs keeps assuring Washington of his pure intentions, whilst that cussed Macdonald of Canada makes no bones about hating Uncle Sam from head to toe."

She allowed that sounded interesting. So he continued. "It's odd to have old Sergeant Foster calling on me down this way. I've worked for and against him up Canada way without official approval from Ottawa. That's where they run Canada from, Ottawa."

She said she knew, and tried in vain to supress a dainty yawn as she said it. So Longarm was tempted to ask her what in blue blazes she *did* want to talk about. Then he

13

wondered why any gent of even his own limited experience with young widow women would want to ask such a dumb question. So, seeing she'd fed him his supper and settled in a love seat with him in the gloaming, he just reached out to haul her in for some friendly spit-swapping as the light through the lace curtains turned from old gold to the ruby glow of smoldering embers.

Despite her nickname, Prune felt soft and squishy enough where a gal was supposed to, and she ran her warm wet tongue around inside his lips to determine that he needed no serious dental work. But as soon as he'd returned the favor and she'd sucked his tongue with vigor, she twisted her face a tad aside and demanded, "What do you think you're up to with that fresh left hand, Custis Long?"

He'd already determined that her silk stockings ended in frilly garters at mid-thigh, but she had a good grip on his wrist, and so he could only guess about higher up as he calmly replied, "The delicate way they put what we're doing would be making love, or commencing to, Miss Prune. I could see you didn't want to discuss the Royal Canadian Mounted Police, and I find discussions of our inevitable obituaries as tedious. But if you don't want to have a more romantic conversation, you only need to tell me once."

She laughed weakly, and let go of his wrist as she decided, "I think you *mean* that! But give a poor girl time to get used to the idea! Do you always move this fast? Most men sort of fiddle about with a young lady's . . . upper body before they slide in to home plate!"

Seeing there was nothing stopping him now, Longarm slid his palm up the inside of a smooth thigh to discover she was wearing nothing at all, save for some moist pubic hair, under her summer-weight black skirts. As she hissed in mingled surprise and desire, Longarm calmly confided that he had it on good authority that few gals got much out of titty-squeezing unless they were lactating.

14

Prune protested, "That's not the point. Allowing a gentleman caller to get fresh with your breasts establishes that you are becoming right fond of one another."

Longarm began to strum her old banjo with two moist fingers as he nibbled her earlobe and asked if that felt as if they might be deadly enemies. She sobbed, and parted her thighs, grabbing his wrist again and thrusting his questing fingers deeper as she moaned, "I just know I'm going to hate myself in the morning, you brute! For I see it's true what they say about the notorious Longarm from down Denver way, and I swear I only meant to satisfy some curiosity without letting things go half this far!"

Longarm swung his bottom off the love seat to kneel between her far-flung thighs as he shucked his frock coat and unbuttoned his fly with the one free hand she'd left him, knowing they were at that delicate stage where a gal was as likely to give in or come ahead of you and tell you to stop.

As a law officer, Longarm knew all too well how much trouble an old boy could get into if he failed to stop when a lady damn well ordered him to stop.

But thanks to a certain skill at banjo-strumming, and her being willing to slide her bare butt towards him over the edge of the love seat, he had his old organ-grinder where they both wanted it, with her thrashing her left thigh up and down his right flank as she sought as good a purchase for that knee as the other one hooked over the grips of his holstered .44–40.

It was at times such as these that a man felt glad he'd loaded only five rounds in the wheel. For he'd sure feel dumb if his gun went off before his pecker during such a private party.

Once they'd broken the ice on her love seat, and picked up a few rug burns after they'd both stripped naked, they wound up in her four-poster in a bedroom facing east into the moonrise. Prune's house had been erected sensibly on its site, with the upstairs bedrooms facing east to cool off all afternoon and face the sunrise, while the kitchen down below faced east, downwind of the prevailing westerlies off the nearby Front Range. It was poor folks, or rich Eastern greenhorns, who erected stables upwind, with kitchen doors and bedroom windows facing into the prevailing winds and afternoon heat, to make for a fly-blown and smelly house and sunbaked bedding still warm to the touch at midnight.

Prune's clean linen sheets were cool, and didn't rumple worth mentioning as they rolled about, making up for lost time alone on that merry-go-round, to hear her tell. That lighter-complected and slightly more junoesque young widow in Denver had already explained to the point of tedium how a woman of independent means had to guard her rich husband's estate against fortune hunters in a world where the law gave a man a lot of say in a wife's finances. That brown-haired gal along Sherman Street near the State Capitol had already confessed she'd have never bedded down with him if she hadn't considered anything as formal as a wedding to such an unsuitable swain ridiculous.

So when Prunella Sloan commenced to go into her own mining properties and beef shares during a pause for breath, Longarm suggested they share a smoke. Gals didn't talk as much when they were smoking, and it helped a man get his second wind if he got his own inhaling and exhaling a mite more regular.

She said she didn't mind, as long as he didn't look at her poor old nipples by match light. So he said he wouldn't, and kept his promise as he got a cheroot going for the two of them.

It was easy. Thanks to the full moon shining in on them he could see her bare tits as plain as they'd likely look in the cold gray light of a High Plains dawn. Her perky nipples looked swell. She was most likely trying to remind him he was supposed to play with them.

So he did, hooking one arm over her bare shoulders

16

to fiddle with a tit in one hand, the cheroot in the other, as she tugged on the hairs on his belly almost hard enough to hurt, demanding in mock anger to hear more about that other widow woman down Denver way.

Longarm put the cheroot to her lips as he replied in a firm, friendly voice, "When next we meet, if ever we meet, and she asks me who I got to fuck up this way, would you really want me describing you and this pretty little tit in clinical detail?"

Prune gasped. "Custis, don't use such vulgar terms for what . . . we've been doing. I was married for almost seven years, and I'd be lying if I said I didn't enjoy this sort of thing a lot with a sweet and loving man. But even though we . . . did it most every night until the angels and a summer fever took him from me, we never, ever called what we were up to . . . you know."

He assured her, "I do know. That's how come I don't meant to ever tell some other lady how I fucked you. As to whether I have ever fucked another living soul, that's betwixt me and them, not you, me, and the lamppost."

She fell into a brooding silence. Lest she cloud up and rain all over him, Longarm said soothingly, "Come this time tomorrow, you're likely to feel glad I ain't no pool-hall kiss-and-tell, Miss Prune. I know what you mean about grabbing for them few golden rings we get to. But it's best to grab 'em and enjoy 'em discreetly. That's what you call it when the neighbors don't know who you've been fucking."

So she laughed like hell, snuffed the cheroot out, and forked a dusky bare limb across him in the moonlight to impale herself on his shaft and go wild on top of him, with moonlight flashing on and off between her wide-spread sweat-slicked thighs while she rolled her head from side to side, black hair all aswirl as she begged and pleaded for him to fuck her, fuck her, fuck her, and never stop.

It wouldn't have been polite to point out that she seemed to be doing all the fucking at the moment. So Longarm just lay there to take his beating like a man.

It didn't hurt at all.

Chapter 3

They'd started so early that by the dawn's early light, if they hadn't restored her youth, they'd settled her nerves to where Prune awkwardly asked him if he'd mind sneaking out the back way ahead of the sunrise lest some nosy neighbor question her good character.

So he got himself and his baggage over to the Burlington Hotel, hired a room to store it all in, and went back downstairs for some serious breakfast to settle the warmed-over coffee and cold biscuits a recovering sex maniac had served him on the run.

He ordered his eggs over fried hash with fresh-perked coffee and glazed donuts on the side. He'd just dug in, seated at a corner table with his back nicely covered, when Crown Sergeant Foster from Fort MacLeod and a younger stranger caught up with him.

The big smooth-shaven Mountie had been a vision in scarlet and gold the last few times they'd brushed. So it was just as well Longarm had been expecting to see Foster in civilian garb. As he and his younger companion joined him, Longarm smiled up at the rusty black suit Foster was wearing and asked, "Did they throw you out, or have you quit to enter the Anglican ministry, Sarge?"

As the two of them sat down across from Longarm,

Foster replied in his usual prim tone, "Neither. Your government and our own agree it may be just as well for us to work with you incognito south of our own border. This would be Deputy Constable Henri Grouleau of Canmont Township, close to the border on the Calgary-Great Falls Trail."

"*Mes amis* call me Hank, by gar," the younger Canadian volunteered.

"A Queen's Own blue-eyed Frog," Foster chimed in, and this didn't seem to bother the French Canadian worth mentioning.

Foster's remark sounded less insulting or inane to a U.S. deputy marshal conversant with recent Canadian history. The first Canadians had been French subjects of assorted kings named Louis, more interested in getting rich than settling a new land. So there'd soon been way more British colonists to the south and, kings tending to feud and fuss a lot, the German Georges running England had wound up running Canada as well.

A lot of French Canadians hadn't cared. One king was as big a pain as the next, and to old Ben Franklin's surprise and chagrin, the French Canadians had sat out the American Revolution or sided with the Tories back East. Such loyal British subjects, however odd they might talk, were considered regular Canadians in Ottawa.

But further west, along and beyond the Red River of the North, old French Canadian or other sorts of white hunters, trappers, or Indian traders had settled down and married up with assimilated Indians of the mostly Chippewa and Plains Cree persuasions.

Nobody much had cared, at first. Rustic Christians of mixed or Métis blood, as the Métis or Red River Breeds described themselves, were some improvement over nomadic Plains Nations as the buffalo and beaver got harder to grab than a neighbor's livestock. The Métis had worked out their own new ways of life, based on what white daddies and Indian mommas had considered right or wrong. They tended to be subsistance hoe-farmers and enterprising traders, roaming far and wide across the High Plains of the Canadian West in their admired "Red River carts," a blend of French peasant and Horse Indian craftsmanship, whipped up with horn-hard rawhide holding things together instead of such iron hardware as a white cartwright might have used.

But wandering the High Plains in their Red River carts hadn't been the problem back in Ottawa. All those Métis families squatting on all that West Canadian land, rent-and-tax-and-title-free, had been the problem.

As the current Macdonald Administration of Canada saw it, a half-ass Indian with maybe a dab of white blood had no more real estate rights than any other Stone Age savage. So, while they were willing to concede *some* such rights to Métis who could read, write, and show they'd been paying taxes on land they'd claimed formally, most of the many Métis now residing on fine cattle, wheat, and railroad land had been ordered to stand aside and quit trying to stunt the growth of Her Majesty's danged Dominion.

The Métis had lost their first revolution a short spell back. Their leader, the well-educated and mostly white Louis Riel, was teaching school in Montana Territory as he licked his wounds, and was no doubt planning another try.

But as Longarm had often told his Mexican pals to the south, he was only sworn to defend and uphold the Constitution and Government of These United States, and sometimes that was enough to keep a lawman mighty busy. So as he reached across the donuts to shake with both of them, Longarm only said, "I've rid that trail from Great Falls to Calgary. I stopped to wet my whistle in the prairie town of Canmont, now that I study on it. There wasn't much of a town there, no offense. They told me the unmarked border ran somewheres near. But the place was mostly a handy trail stop offering summer grass and year-round water. Has somebody robbed the bank in Canmont, gents?"

Foster disdainfully replied, "They don't have a bank in Canmont, and we've warned them Her Majesty would like visitors to sign her guest book, coming or going."

Hank Grouleau protested, "Her Majesty she no pay anyone in Canmont to regard her borders! How many times we have to say such *choses* form no part of *l'ordre* in a village the size of Canmont, *hein*?"

Foster replied in the fluent French of a serious learner, "*Mais non, et non jeter de la poudre aux yeux* and speak English, you fucking Frog! We're in Fort Collins, Colorado, not the south of France where the women wear no pants!"

Grouleau replied with some indignation that his family had arrived from Normandie, and added, "I was only trying to say that regarding the border is hardly the duty of an informally elected constabulary, and did we not arrest that species of a renegade nun when she try to slip past us after dark?"

Foster grimaced and declared, "Another example of Gallic wit. The murderous little snip would have surely made it, had she been content to rein in for beer and water at the regular crossing before riding on. You have your federal warrant on you at the moment, don't you, Deputy Long?"

Longarm washed down the last of his hash and signaled the waiter for three fresh mugs of coffee as he nodded with a puzzled smile. He confided, "I have to pack some identification out in the field. Sometimes the badge pinned in my wallet ain't enough for the local law."

Foster asked if Longarm would show his standard government form to the semi-professional Canadian deputy.

Longarm shrugged, got out his wallet, and removed the warrant tucked behind the flap of his badge. He

22

dunked a donut as Hank Grouleau spread the high-school-diploma-sized federal warrant on the table to read:

KNOW ALL MEN BY THESE PRESENTS:

THAT I, WILLIAM VAIL, Marshal of the United States for the Denver District Court of Colorado, reposing special trust and confidence in CUSTIS LONG—of West Virginia by way of Denver, Colorado—in said federal district, have constituted and appointed, and by these presents do constitute and appoint him, the said CUSTIS LONG—DEPUTY MARSHAL OF THE UNITED STATES FOR THE DENVER DISTRICT COURT OF COLORADO

Under Me, The Said Marshal

AND I DO HEREBY GRANT UNTO HIM, the said CUSTIS LONG full power and authority as my Deputy Marshal throughout the said district to use and exercise the said office of Deputy Marshal according to the laws and custom of the United States relative to and pertaining to duties of a Deputy Marshal during my term of office unless he shall legally be discharged from them. . . .

From there it just ran down into things the French-speaking Canadian felt no call to bother with.

As Foster ignored Longarm's silent offer of some donuts, Grouleau handed the warrant back and decided, "They both seem much the same, *avec* of course the different points of origin. This other deputy U.S. marshal, she show warrant from Fort Smith in your Indian Territory, him."

Longarm folded his own documentation away as he decided, "That don't sound right. Not a court order of any kind from a Fort Smith in an Indian Territory, not

23

the way you said it. Fort Smith has jurisdiction *over* the nearby Indian Territory. It ain't *in* no Indian Territory. The Five Civilized Tribes would weep and wail if a federal court located on another tribe's reserve got to lord it over the other four. Fort Smith's in the Federal District of Western Arkansas. Presided over at the moment by Judge Isaac Parker, and I understand he has over a hundred deputies out policing the Indian Territory as we speak. But he'd never issue a warrant *from* the Indian Territory. Say what you like about old Ike's community gallows in Fort Smith, nobody has ever accused him of sloppy bookkeeping. He dots every I and crosses every T when he signs a death sentence or any other legal document."

Grouleau accepted a donut with a nod of thanks as Foster shot him a dirty look and said, "Canmont could have checked by wire. They never thought to, and they had Sister Simone locked up!"

Grouleau dunked and growled, "*Merde!* How many times must we have this *tres fatigue* discussion, *hein*? I have tell you I only speak to this species of *equivoque* the one time. When she ask me about our prisoner, him, I say she should speak to Marshal LeClerc, him!"

Longarm blinked and decided, "I reckon I should have got more sleep last night. If you gents can't talk English, could you talk just a tad slower? Who's this Sister Simone and are we talking about him or her?"

Foster laughed despite himself and explained, "Hank means the rider who came in to claim Sister Simone was a man. Don't ask me why Frog Canucks call everything a she up front and explain later on whether they mean he or she. I've studied French. I mean real French. Not the *langue verte* or Quebecois our Frog Canucks call French."

Grouleau blazed, "*Sacre bleu! Mais non!* Our Quebecois, she is the *langue du Roi* as was spoke before

24

the end of civilization during that *debacle du bastille* we take no part in!"

Foster sighed and said, "Oh, do shut up and let me do the talking. We haven't come all this way to give this Yankee lawman either history or French lessons, eh, what?"

Longarm was too polite to say that was about the most sensible thing he'd ever heard Crown Sergeant Foster say.

Seeing he had the floor in spite of being seated across from the two of them, Foster said, "Let's start at the beginning, some miles north of the border crossing at Canmont. Sister Simone, as you just now guessed, would seem to be female. After that, opinions vary as to whether she's a renegade nun who ran off with the church plate and a defrocked priest, the sister of some Métis gang leader, or as some of her Cree associates would have it, an *esquawendigo*. I understand that's a Plains Nation version of the Irish Banshee?"

Longarm nodded and said, "Wendigo Woman. Wendigo don't translate as easy as evil fairy or ogre. Is this Sister Simone an Indian or mayhaps a breed?"

Foster dryly replied, "I mean to ask her, before they hang her. As I just said, some rumors tie her in with the Métis movement of that old half-breed ogre Louis Riel. Others say she's of pure Tinker or Irish Gypsy descent. Rome has been of little help in the matter. The Papists in Quebec tend to give Her Majesty's Government evasive answers about what goes on inside their convents. Damned if I see why."

Longarm exchanged knowing glances with the French Canadian Grouleau. Longarm knew better than to waste breath discussing the Bill of Rights with an Anglo-Canadian brought up under Queen Victoria. He knew, and didn't need another lecture from Foster about it, how a younger Queen Victoria had insisted her new government do away with chattel slavery more than twenty years before Lincoln's Emancipation Proclamation, and a lot of Englishmen seemed sincerely confused by Irish resentment left over from just a few hundred years of persecution. For hadn't their Good Queen Vickie repealed those laws passed under Good Queen Bess, and how was anyone to sort out the property deeds of impoverished families and burned out churches at *this* late date?

As if he'd read Longarm's more republican mind, Foster declared, "I was rather hoping you might be able to get more along those lines from the Papist priests you drink with down in Denver, eh, what?"

Longarm dryly remarked, "I have found it easier to talk to folks of other faiths when you don't call them drunks, dolly worshipers, or bead mumblers. Informants of the Hebrew persuasion seem more willing to talk to a canvasing lawman who refrains from calling them Christ killers, and I've found most Mormons would rather be called Latter-day Saints than thieving sex maniacs. Leaving aside just how our Sister Simone might have started out, what's she been up to that calls for an international woman hunt?"

Foster answered without hesitation, "Murder in the first, highway robbery, inciting to riot, and endangering the morals of Her Majesty's Indian subjects. We understand she and her ragtag gang of border ruffians have run guns and firewater to those Sioux and Cheyenne who fled north after Little Big Horn as well. Have I ever told you what we think of your Indian policy, Longarm?"

The laconic Longarm muttered, "Many a time, and I still say it ain't up to me or even my boss, Billy Vail, to set Indian policy on either side of the damned border. Get to the part about this Sister Simone and some fella waving a fake deputy's warrant . . . where? In Canmont, on the border?"

Foster nodded grimly and said, "They *had* her. They'd picked her up on suspicion of vagrancy and—"

"How come?" Longarm cut in. "I mean, what was she doing as made folks suspicious of her on the High Plains in greenup when all sorts of riders are roaming the range in casual dress? Was the gal dressed up like a hobo, a nun, or an Indian evil spirit?"

When Foster confirmed Longarm's guess that they'd spotted a strange young woman dressed Métis, in that curious mixture of French peasant and Horse Indian, Longarm allowed he hadn't pictured her in a nun's habit.

Foster said, "We live in troubled times, and you can load a lot of guns in a Red River cart. She was driving one alone, albeit with two saddle broncs tethered to the tailgate. When they searched her cart they found no guns or firewater. She was obviously on her way south to buy some. She had over a hundred in cash and a strongbox of loot from the robbery of the Calgary Mail Coach. So they brought her in and wired us at Fort MacLeod. We told them to hold her until we could send someone down for her."

He shot Hank Grouleau a disgusted look and said, "This so-called U.S. deputy marshal from Fort Smith got there first. In addition to his own false identification, he produced a prior arrest warrant from the Indian Territory, claiming Sister Simone as a renegade missionary who'd run off with some tribal funds, and this lad's late superior, Constable LeClerc, handed her over without hesitation!"

Longarm asked how Grouleau's boss had gotten to be late.

The younger deputy said, "She got fired, him. I was not there, but from all I have heard, was a, how you say, open-and-shut case of *le droit du plus fort, hein*?"

Foster volunteered, "He means might makes right. This blustering self-styled lawman simply waited until Constable LeClerc was all alone for the evening, then declared he'd ridden many a mile to bring a U.S. federal want back dead or alive, and meant to clean the plow of any son of a bitch who stood in the way of his rough justice."

Foster relented and reached for a donut as he added, "To be fair, as Hank here says, the whole three-man force combined would hardly add up to one serious gunslick, and they do say your Bat Masterson is a gunslick to be reckoned with !"

Longarm stared thunderstruck at the two Canadians as he tried to decide whether they were funning him. When he saw they seemed serious, he laughed and asked, "Before we go on, could I interest either of you greenhorns in my mining claim out back? They got it piled high with horse manure at the moment, but I reckon I could throw in a shovel."

Chapter 4

When he saw he couldn't sell the two Canadians a Colorado mining claim under a pile of shit, Longarm leaned back to fish out three smokes as he said, "You gents have come to the right source after all. I can tell you right now that your fake U.S. marshal was most likely another Canadian, like your Sister Simone herself."

"You mean she was not the real Bat Masterson, him?" asked Hank Grouleau.

Longarm said, "Not hardly. The two surviving Masterson brothers, James and Bartholomew or Bat, have never to this day served as U.S. deputy marshals. That's possibly because neither was American-born. The whole bunch hailed from *Canada* to begin with. Jim's the more serious town-tamer. But Bat has the handle the reporters fancy. Last I heard, Bat was here in Colorado, down Trinidad way. How do you like another Canadian knowing this and taking advantage of the real Bat Masterson's rep, knowing he'd hardly be likely to surface in Calmont during a one-night stand?"

Foster asked, "Do you know the real Bat Masterson? Can you get in touch with him for us?"

Longarm nodded, but asked, "What for? You don't suspect *him* of aiding and abetting a jailbreak in Canmont from way the hell down in Trinidad, do you?"

Foster said, "No. But he might have some idea who'd impersonate a Canadian shootist to rescue a Canadian bad woman, wouldn't he?"

Lighting Grouleau's cheroot for him, Longarm confided to the French Canadian, "Foster's always been that way, ever since first we met, not far from here in the South Pass country. I had a hunting hound like that one time when I was a kid. Damned if I recall whatever happened to that old hound. It just ran sniffing and woofing in all directions till, one day, it just run off for good."

He shook out the match stem and added, "Never did catch a rabbit or even a coon with that impetuous woofer."

Foster declined to smoke with them as he demanded, "Very well, just where might *you* start sniffing for the renegade nun and that impostor?"

Longarm got his own smoke going before he decided, "Not even farther from where they were last seen, Sarge. Has anyone established they rid as far south as Great Falls, and by the way, what ever happened to that Red River cart she'd been driving?"

Foster said, "It's been impounded as evidence, of course. The fake Yank lawman who rode off into the night with her—those handcuffs were a nice touch—apparently brought some riding stock north with him. He might or might not have had some others out on the prairie to back his play and assist in the getaway. By the time one of our own mounted officers from Fort MacLeod arrived, their trail was stone-cold under at least two spring rains. The Montana territorials and some deputies from your Helena Federal District went through some motions, of course. But the first break we've had happened here in Fort Collins. An expensive but engraved watch turned up in a pawnshop down the street. An alert jeweler I shall never call a Christ killer recognized it, a tad too late, from some lists of stolen goods he goes over in his spare time. We just got here. So neither of us has spoken to him as yet, but—"

"Jesus H. Christ!" Longarm cut in, catching their waiter's eyes and signaling for the tab before he polished off his coffee and rose to his considerable height. "What in tarnation have we been doing at this infernal table when there's a real live *witness* in town to canvas?"

As they legged it along the walk in the now-bright morning sunlight, Foster explained how his own office had been keeping him informed by wire. Longarm said he'd figured out what the three of them were doing there in Fort Collins finally. Young Grouleau seemed to be getting a kick out of hearing somebody fussing at Foster for a change. Foster was enough of an old pro not to stand on ceremony. He'd agreed to go along with having a Colorado rider on this woman hunt simply because on more than one occasion in the past their different approaches to law and order had meshed rather neatly in the end. Had Crown Sergeant Foster of the RCMP even considered what a kid deputy might think of him, he'd have decided he didn't *give* a grasshopper's fart.

The pawnshop was near the loading docks where down-and-out stockyard hands tended to gather, and was open for business, cluttered with everything from buffalo guns to bass drums and presided over by a total surprise.

The Widow Sadie Kramer, as she introduced herself, stood around five feet two, with blue eyes, a little button nose, curly hair the color of a Colorado sunset, and a Yiddish accent you could cut with a knife. She was wearing a denim smock over a summer frock of pongee or light tan wild silk. When they told her who they were and what they wanted with her, she turned a hanging sign in her glass-topped door to declare the place closed, and led them on back to her private quarters at the rear. Her kitchen window and open back door overlooked a neatly kept jungle of closely planted salad greens and giant sunflower stalks that had some growing left in them that early in the season.

She made the three of them sit around her kitchen table as she rustled up a heroic snack of kosher pilaf while she explained how she'd thought there was something funny about that couple, but how do you run back here for your lists with nobody watching them up front?

As she proceeded to dole out the aromatic pilaf she seemed to keep simmering in endless supply, Crown Sergeant Foster protested that he'd eaten aboard the morning train.

Sadie Kramer insisted, "So eat again and you won't get hungry so soon. How can anybody be expected to think on an empty stomach? Do you see *me* thinking on an empty stomach?"

Longarm decided not to comment on a mighty trim waistline despite her brag. He got along better than Sergeant Foster with immigrants from other parts because he could see different folks had different ways of acting friendly. He'd sometimes wondered how friendly his own kind seemed to others, since Anglo-Saxons let a caller just sit there with no more than a cup of coffee and a slice of cake. Everybody else from Arapaho to Zuni seemed to feel they had to stuff you full. Such notions likely came from memories of hungry times in other parts. He knew Irish folks who could remember when one boiled potato was a real treasure, and he'd heard how wild some folks from the Russian Pale got over sunflower seeds. So he dug into his bowl of pilaf like a good sport, and it wasn't half bad, if only he hadn't been so full of hash and glazed donuts. Pilaf was sort of like grits, only tastier.

To excuse himself from not swallowing, Longarm asked the pawnshop owner what she'd meant about the couple who'd pawned that watch looking funny.

Sadie Kramer seemed as glad for the excuse to set her own spoon aside as she replied, "Not *dressed* funny.

Dressed, they looked like you and me and the people across the street. He was about forty, wore a derby, and should get more exercise. She was maybe thirty, trying for sixteen in a cheap but well-fitting calico frock. Black hair and oily skin she should wash with soap more often. Hair pinned up for public streets in daytime, but trying to break loose, like snakes already. Confidental, I don't think she washes her hair much either."

"Were they both . . . ah, Christians?" asked Foster awkwardly.

Sadie Kramer sniffed and shot back, "I should ask? This is Fort Collins, Colorado, not Frankfurt or Krakow already. But since *you* had to ask, I'll tell you, a Roman Catastrophe she had to be."

"What makes you say that?" asked Foster.

Their Jewish hostess answered simply, "She said so. Not right out. 'Confidential, I'm a Roman Catastrophe.' But who else would tell some gonif in a derby she was running for one of *those places* with her own share? They didn't know I could hear so good when I'm bent down to get money out of a bottom drawer. You shouldn't leave all your money in one drawer when you run a pawnshop alone since your man was taken, may he rest in peace."

Before Foster could do so rudely, Longarm gently cut in. "What sort of places do you figure a Roman Catholic outlaw gal might run for, Miss Sadie?"

The petite redhead answered simply, "Where they keep those girls dressed up like penguins, of course. Don't they call them nunces or something?"

Longarm nodded and said, "Close enough. This oily black-headed gal pawning a stolen watch told her derby-hatted confederate she was headed for some *convent*?"

"I don't know. What's a convent?" the obvious non-Catholic replied.

When Longarm explained a convent was where Catholic nuns hung out, she brightened and said, "That sounds right. Now that I think back she called it something like a *numeral!*"

"Nunnery?" asked Foster with an uncertain smile.

When she agreed that sounded better, Foster told Longarm, "British usage. You Yanks and the Irish Papists use the term convent more. I say, I think that just may be a clue!"

Hank Grouleau volunteered, "If they were Quebecois-speaking Metís, one would expect her to run home to *la abbaye, non?*"

Foster smiled wolfishly and asked Sadie Kramer if there was a nunnery, convent, or whatever there in Fort Collins.

She laughed and replied, "You're asking *me*? It's enough I should know where the *shul* might be if ever I believe again! All I can tell you about that pair is that they came in with that nice watch and a few less valuable items. I got the feeling they were hard up for cash, and to tell the truth, I was more worried about getting robbed than I cared about where they were going. I let them have twenty on the watch. Only because it was better I should lose on the deal than wind up on the floor with a bump. After they left, I got out those lists of stolen merchandise, and how often does a mother inscribe a graduation watch to a son named *My Galahad* already?"

She caught the exchanged looks between the two Canadians, and asked Longarm, "So I was warm? Those two are wanted for something really important?"

Longarm told her, "Mighty important, ma'am, and thanks to you, we may have cut a cold trail a lot closer to their tails than they were figuring when they decided they'd packed that loot far enough. How long ago did you say they came by with that stuff from a mail coach robbery, ma'am?"

She looked like a little gal unwrapping presents now, as she told them the mysterious couple had pawned the watch two days before yesterday and that she'd put it out on the wire within an hour of discovery.

That gave the men the excuse to pass on the rest of all that pilaf. As they were leaving to scout for the nearest convent, Sadie Kramer asked if they'd come back and tell her as soon as they found anything worth repeating. So Longarm assured her he would, and ticked his hat brim to her as he was the last one out her door.

Out on the walk, Crown Sergeant Foster stiffly observed it was best not to promise anything to a witness, once he or she had given all the information they might have.

Longarm shrugged and said, "You never know how much a witness may or may not know, Sarge. I like to keep the folks I jaw with feeling neighborly. I've had 'em come in the next day, or later, remembering something they forgot the first time."

Foster sniffed and said, "She spotted a very unusual inscription on an expensive watch. After that she couldn't tell a Roman Catholic from a Roman *Catastrophe*, for God's sake!"

Longarm said, "Ignorant ain't the same as dumb. She did overhear the gal say she was headed on home to her convent, and if that ain't a good lead, I don't know what you'd call it!"

Some Irish-looking gents were coming along the walk towards them. Longarm stopped them with a friendly smile to ask if they could tell him the way to the convent in Fort Collins.

The two local men looked sincerely puzzled. One said, "Sure and I know of no such establishment up this way, young sir. Are you sure it ain't the grand convent school of Saint Barbara's in Denver you'd be after seeking?"

Longarm settled for the name and location of their nearest Papist church. As they three lawman moved towards that central hub of Fort Collins, Foster decided, "I can't see any priest knowing more about Sister Simone's true identity or present whereabouts than that Kramer woman back at the pawnshop."

The French Canadian Grouleau decided, "Not as much, *mes amis*. They did not know they were being overheard in the shop. I do not think a priest, she is going to hear that much from Sister Simone, him. Sister Simone does not sound like a *femme* who goes to confession *très* often, *hein*?"

Longarm smiled thinly and replied, "I'm still trying to get some notion of what she *looks* like. Did you get a good look at her up to Canmont when they first arrested her?"

To which Grouleau modestly replied, "*Oui,* I was one of the riders who arrested her. She was drive, how you say, lickety-spittle over rolling prairie at nightfall. Our first concern was that she seemed about to kill herself. Once we stopped her, and regarded how she kept changing her story, and fitting the description of Sister Simone, eh, bien, it followed as the night the day."

Foster confided, "I only put up with him because he knows the mad bitch on sight. None of the others on the Canmont force are worth the powder to blow them to hell! They *had* her, *cold,* and let that lover boy ride off with her, laughing like a loon, I'll vow!"

The three of them paused on the corner to let a beer dray pass before they crossed over. Longarm found himself near a wooden Indian, and remembered he was getting low on smokes. As he turned that way, Foster paused to ask why he'd stopped. Hank Grouleau stepped off the plank walk and strode two paces out across the packed clay and horseshit before a high-powered .51-caliber round took him high in his left rib cage to explode out the far side in a gory eruption of bone splinters and torn flesh before it spanged off a lamppost to scream off in the distance with a banshee wail.

As Grouleau crumpled like a busted balloon, Foster yelled, "To your left! Rooftop!"

So Longarm had no call to answer as he ran that way with Foster hot on his heels, panting, "You take the front stairs and I'll take the back and let's *get* the flaming bastard!"

Chapter 5

They didn't. Since they'd both spotted the same gun smoke above a flat-roofed four-families-two-shops tenement, Longarm barged in through the front door between a barbershop and hardware store to charge up the inside stairs, .44-40 in hand, while Sergeant Foster ran around to the back to move up the open rear stairwell. The two lawmen met atop the graveled tar-paper roof. You could still smell the kitchen-match odor of spent black powder, but the rooftop sniper hadn't left so much as a brass cartridge behind.

Down below a shrill voice called out, "I see you two up on that roof! What are you two doing up on that roof? You'd better tell me what you two are doing up on that roof right this instant, hear?"

Longarm holstered his six-gun and broke out his wallet as he strode to the knee-high parapet to flash his badge down at the gathering crowd below. A badge flashed back in the clear Colorado sunlight, and that same voice called up, "I would be City Marshal Rubin Hawthorn and what can you tell me about this dead body down by the corner?"

Longarm, called down, "He was with us. I'd be U.S.

Deputy Marshal Custis Long, and I sure could use some help securing this tenement, pard!"

The town law asked what Longarm wanted them to do. He told them. As Hawthorn and his own deputies fanned out to canvas all the flats within easy dashing distance for uninvited guests, Longarm turned to Foster with a fatalistic smile to say, "What can I tell you? We could get lucky. But it's just as likely the son of a bitch had his getaway route mapped out in advance. It ain't as if this was a sudden impulse."

"What makes you so smug and sure?" asked the Mountie in mufti as he put his own .455 back in its shoulder rig. As Longarm stared at him bemused, Foster demanded, "What did I say now? Haven't you ever heard of criminal impulses, Yank?"

Longarm said, "There was nothing impulsive about this setup. They were expecting us. They were *waiting* for us here in Fort Collins."

"How do you know that?" Foster demanded. "How could they have possibly known Sadie Kramer had reported that stolen watch or—oh, I say, that *does* sound rather sneaky!"

Longarm nodded grimly and said, "I was wondering how come such successful outlaws would stoop to hocking jewelry for petty cash. Sadie Kramer herself suggested how easy it would be for a pair of stone-cold killers to rob her, and they'd held back that other robbery loot!"

"They *expected* her to spot that stolen watch!" Foster marveled as the two of them headed for the back stairs.

Longarm growled, "That's about the size of it. A kid pickpocket would expect an expensive watch with such an unusual inscription to be reported. They knew you knew that watch had been stolen up your way by Sister Simone's bunch. So they knew you, poor Grouleau, and some fool like me would show up at Sadie Kramer's pawnshop in a bunch, as we just did, to head back to the hub together, through the field of fire they chose well in advance, as we just did!"

As they headed down the inside stairs by mutual silent assent, they met town lawmen coming the other way in a room-by-room search of the premises. As they passed on down, Foster grudgingly conceded, "Hank Grouleau was their most important target. Neither you nor I would be able to recognize Sister Simone on sight. I've never seen her in the flesh."

They were out on the street again when the penny dropped and Longarm asked, "What do you mean by in the flesh? Have you ever seen at least a *picture* of the sneaky bitch?"

Neither had to tell the other where they were headed next as the burly Mountie in mufti replied, "Just a sepia-tone of three nuns having quite a party. The one with the neck of a wine bottle shoved up inside her is reputed to be the one and original Sister Simone. We don't know who the other two were, but it seems as if they were having a girlish orgy in one of their cells, judging by the alarmingly realistic crucifix on the stucco wall above the cot they're sharing. Our Lord seemed quite disturbed by the proceedings."

Longarm made a wry face and asked, "How could you tell they were nuns if they were throwing a bare-ass orgy with bottles and such?"

They were elbowing their way through the crowd around the fallen deputy Grouleau now, so Foster chose his words as he quietly explained, "They weren't completely . . . out of uniform. Sister Simone and another still wore their rosaries and wimples as they . . . misbehaved. The other was wearing the full habit of a teaching order, according to another Canadian who was more conversant on such Papish matters."

A sawbones and some meat-wagon attendants had rolled the kid they were talking about aboard a litter. When Foster asked which hospital they were taking him to, the sawbones quietly replied, "He's beyond any need of a hospital. They'll be taking him to the morgue on College Avenue. If he's important to you, you'll have to take it up with the coroner's office."

Foster turned to Longarm to demand, "*Do* something, Yank! We can't have a Canadian lawman in a perishing Colorado grave!"

As they proceeded to load the cadaver aboard the horse-drawn ambulance, Longarm said soothingly, "They ain't fixing to bury nobody. They'll keep him on ice till after an autopsy. Then they'll release him to a local undertaker of your choice. You'll want him embalmed and sealed in a lead-lined box before you ship him far with summer coming on. I sure would like to see that picture of Sister Simone enjoying herself like so."

Foster said he'd have to send to Fort MacLeod for a copy, adding, "It's not the sort of picture a gentleman would want to have in his pocket if he was run over by a train. I doubt it would be of much use to us in any case. Her hair is hidden under her wimple and one lewdly grinning little brunette looks much the same as any other in grainy shades of brown and white."

"What's she built like?" asked Longarm.

Foster shrugged and said, "Like a little brunette who ought to be ashamed of herself. No distinguishing marks. Well-formed but average-sized breasts, with a bit more pubic hair than usual, if that's what you're after."

Longarm mildly suggested, "I thought we were all after *her,* and how come you said she was only *reputed* to be a renegade nun if you have a picture of her throwing an orgy in a convent?"

"*If* it was a convent and those other two were really nuns," Foster pointed out. As the ambulance drove off with the remains of the only Roman Catholic in the three-man posse, Foster said, "There's a French-postcard feel to that bawdy picture. As if it had been taken for public consumption. The three girls obviously held still long enough for an indoor exposure. Only one of them had a complete nun's habit, and the other stage props would be even easier to come by."

"You mean you think it was staged to form mayhaps a whole set of them French postcards mostly packaged in York State?" asked Longarm as a whole new pattern suddenly suggested itself.

Foster said, "I have to follow poor Grouleau down to the morgue and throw some of Her Majesty's weight about. Don't ask me where they took that dirty picture of Sister Simone, if it's really a picture of Sister Simone. As to the setting, we've all seen those pictures of a well-endowed Moor having his wicked way with a blond captive in his wicked harem. I submit there may be Arabesque wallpaper and well-hung colored stevedores closer than the shores of Tripoli."

"You're saying the wicked lady we're after could be no more than a common whore." Longarm nodded. It hadn't been a question.

As Longarm stood in place in his stovepipe boots, Foster asked, "Aren't you coming?"

Longarm shook his head and said, "I'll meet you later at our hotel. Poor old Hank ain't fixing to tell us anything new about that gal he arrested up your way. But whilst we're on the subject, did you ever show him that picture of Sister Simone?"

Foster asked, "How did you think I knew that fully dressed nun was wearing a teaching sister's habit? I confess he seemed less sure about the blurred image of Sister Simone herself. He said she *looked* like the dark stranger he'd brought in off the range after sundown. But he said a *lot* of naked women on French postcards looked something like that. Where did you say you were going?"

"Back along the same trail." Longarm sighed, adding, "If they set us up, they knew we were coming. The only way they could have known we were coming was on account they'd *invited* us to come, see?"

Foster grimaced and said, "Bring me some pilaf for a late snack. I hope you've considered that that bloke with the buffalo rifle may still be in town."

"He's lost the advantage of surprise," Longarm pointed out, patting his holstered .44–40 as he almost purred, "I hope he ain't figured that out yet. How long do you figure you'll be with poor old Hank?"

Foster thought and decided, "Let's give one another some slack and agree to meet at the Burlington House around supper time."

They shook on it and parted company. Longarm ambled back to Sadie Kramer's pawnshop as Foster followed the ambulance on foot.

Longarm found the little redhead in her open front doorway. When she spied him, she gasped, "Oy! It was somebody else they shot! I heard the shot from here! A boy running by just now said they'd shot a lawman! Come inside before they shoot another already!"

He did, and again she closed her shop and locked the front door as she made clucking sounds and suddenly burst into tears like a scared little kid.

So Longarm hauled her against his rough tobacco-tweed vest to softly say, "Easy does it, Miss Sadie. I was there and it wasn't scary as all *that*. Nobody's fixing to harm a single red hair on your pretty little skull, see?"

She sobbed, "A lot you know! My Morris said there was nothing for me to worry about. You men are all alike! You're all going to live forever and then we get to clean up the blood!"

She pulled away enough to point dramatically at a spot on the floor near the caged counter and sobbed, "Pints he bled! Quarts he bled! Who knew such a skinny man could have so much blood in him?"

"Was it a holdup as turned ugly?" Longarm quietly asked, without letting go.

She buried her snub nose in his tweed and replied, "He reported a pair of silver-mounted and monogrammed spurs to the sheriff's office. He had to. It's the law. The rich stockman they'd murdered and robbed had been wearing those same spurs. This was in the papers already, and so when this young gonif came in to pawn the same spurs, what was my Morris to do? It's the law already."

She went on to explain how her late husband's report had led to an arrest and conviction. But they'd only nabbed one of the gang, and his hanging wasn't going to do the late Morris Kramer any good. One or more of the outlaw's pals had come by at quitting time, and his widow had had to put the rest together from the sounds of gunplay up front.

As she finished, she sobbed, "What if that Catastrophe couple who pawned that watch come back to shoot me for reporting it?"

Longarm truthfully replied, "They ain't likely to, Miss Sadie. I am just about certain they *expected* you to report *My Galahad*'s graduation watch. They'd likely heard about your late husband's gallant death and banked on you being as brave. They never wanted your twenty dollars. They wanted you to help 'em bait a hook, and since you did just what they wanted you to do for them, they'd have no call to seek revenge."

"Easy for you to say. You weren't here," she pointed out.

He said, "I know. That's why I came back. You know who Sister Simone is supposed to be. I'm trying to get a better picture. On the one hand she's supposed to be one thing, and on the other hand she ain't. I just now heard they may have a picture that may have been taken in a convent when the mother superior wasn't watching. It could have just as easily been taken somewheres else. Sister Simone sure don't behave like a paid-up member of an RC teaching order. On the other hand, we have a picture of her in their habit, sort of, and you did say you'd heard her tell that cuss in the derby she was headed on home to her convent, right?"

Sadie pointed again and said, "While I was bending over out of sight behind that counter already."

Longarm nodded and said, "I'd like you to help me out with a sort of experiment, ma'am. Could you go back behind your counter and bend over the same way for me?"

She pulled away, blushing, to murmur, "Such a question with the two of us alone in here! How often do you ask women to bend over with head and shoulders so low and tush so high?"

Longarm smiled at the mental picture and said, "I won't peek. I'll stand right here and tell this other gent in the derby that I'm off to a nunnery, if that was what she said."

The little redhead dimpled up at him and decided, "So he's a *goy* and a little *meshuggah* besides, but a good heart, so why not?"

She opened a flap to get behind her caged counter and drop out of sight as she giggled. "Oy, if you could see me now! So something is supposed to happen next?"

Longarm softly murmured, "Yep, from here I'm headed home to my old nunnery. Did you hear that, Miss Sadie?"

She called back, "Of course I heard it. Did I say I was deaf?"

He tried it in a whisper. Sadie Kramer proved to have sharper ears than some when she was able to hear that, and some nonsense poetry he threw in just to make sure.

When he told her she'd more than satisfied him, she smiled coyly through the brass bars at him and replied, "Speak for yourself. Are you married? Do you have someone steady on the side?"

He laughed and said, "Not here in Collins, Miss Sadie. They sent me here to put naughty young gals in jail. But that ain't saying I ain't open to other suggestions—once I get some free time, I mean. As of the moment I'd rather talk some more about them treacherous Canadian outlaws who used you to bait a death trap here in Collins."

She opened the flap and said, "So come in the back with me already and first we'll fuck and then we can talk!"

Chapter 6

"Oy! What am I doing up here at this hour?" Sadie Kramer exclaimed as Longarm lowered her to the covers of her second-story four-poster a tad early for his usual noon dinner. So he asked her if she wanted him to stop.

But she threw her little arms around his neck to draw him down to her as she protested, "I only asked what I was doing up here at this hour. Did you hear me ask you to stop?"

So he laughed, kissed her fondly, and the next time she asked him what she was doing, he allowed they called it screwing back in West-by-God-Virginia.

She said in that case she wanted to take all her duds off and do it right. So he rolled off just long enough to shuck his own duds while she stripped down to her pretty little buff and got on top.

Sadie had one of those compact baby-doll bodies too solid to call chubby and too soft to call chunky. As she bounced atop him, her red hair came unbound to fall down the front of her so her firmly bounding nipples could play hide-and-seek with him as she braced her palms flat against his bare chest to twist and turn while she moved her old ring-dang-do up and down, complimenting him or fussing at him in Yiddish. It was hard to say which when a gal got that excited.

She suddenly climaxed with a surprised, muffled scream of pleased surprise. Then she collapsed atop him as limp as a dishrag to weep and wail that she'd never meant to be such a *verrucktefrau* and maybe she should see a doctor for her nerves.

Longarm hadn't finished coming in her, so he rolled her on her back and spread her short, shapely legs wide with an elbow braced under either calf so they had no need for a pillow under her well-rounded little rump as he threw some serious effort into her.

As he did so, Sadie pleaded, "Not again! What kind of a *shlomp* do you take me for? We've done it already and . . ."

Then she decided, "And I want to do it some more! I can't believe I just said that! Who taught you to do it so many times in a row, you *meshuggah mensch*?"

He wasn't sure how you answered that. So he just kept pounding her till he came, and then, seeing she was panting so hard and moving so nice under him, he figured he'd just come again.

She seemed to like it while it lasted. But then she turned on the water taps as they lay together atop her rumpled covers in the balmy afternoon breeze off her back garden.

As he got a cheroot going to share with her, Sadie sobbed, "I know you won't believe this, but I've only been like this with one other man since my Morris was murdered. I'm not sure he was expecting me to get crazy either. We've never spoken about it since I sent him home to his wife. Do you believe in Gehenna? I think your people call it Hell."

Longarm shrugged a bare shoulder under her tousled red waves as he replied, "I have my doubts. The Good Book holds that a Just God loves us poor little puny critters he created in His Image. So can you picture a just and loving creator allowing most men and women less than a hundred years to figure right from wrong and feeling *that* sore at 'em for messing up their mayfly lives?"

She sniffed and said, "Certainly. Look what happened to the cities on the plain, and Lot's wife only turned around for a little peek! So what do you think they'll do to me in Gehenna for having no control over myself down there? If I told you half the things I've shoved in there for my nerves, you'd never want you should have your *shmuckela* in me no more! I just can't help myself when these feelings come over me whenever I get excited!"

He saw she didn't want a drag on his cheroot. So he set a smoke ring adrift in the sunlight above their bare bodies and suggested, "Try not to get excited then. Or find a steadier soother than a married man or tumbleweed lawman. Married-up friends tell me it's a wonder how such nervous feelings subside as soon as you have somebody near at hand to sooth 'em."

He took another drag, chuckled, and continued. "I know this old boy used to get in bar fights and ride twelve miles into town to get . . . his nerves soothed of a Saturday night. Then he married up with a pretty schoolmarm, and of late he's been complaining that she keeps after him to come to bed early when he's in the middle of a swell book."

She sighed and said, "Morris used to stay up late building ships in bottles. One night when my nerves were bothering me, Morris told me how he'd wanted to be a sailor when he grew up. I understood him better already after that. When I was little, there was this field of sunflowers near our *shtetl,* in the old country. Sunflowers as far as you could see already, and I wanted I should run barefoot through such a field, all the way to the horizon, singing. But such singing was not meant for girls like me."

He suggested, "You might have got stung by bees in

a field full of sunflower seeds, Miss Sadie. I noticed your swell garden out back. So what's to stop you from filing on a quarter section under the Homestead Act and growing enough sunflowers to get that dream out of your system?"

She told him he was talking like a *shlemiel*. Others of her faith had confided to him the meaning of the Yiddish endearment. He insisted, "I grew up on a hardscrabble farm in the hills of West-by-God-Virginia, and I would have been a fool to stay there, trying to grow enough corn to matter at a forty-five-degree angle. The grass is ever greener on the other side of the fence, and there are dusted out homesteaders a day's ride from here who'd say you were living high on the hog with your own shop under a roof that don't leak."

She said, "Before they murdered him, Morris and me wasted breath on talking about your Homestead Act. He said sometimes he felt like running away to sea, joining a circus, or becoming a cowboy when he grew up. But all of us are born to be what our people have always been. Like it or lump it."

Longarm caressed her soft flank, seeing it was so handy, as he gently asked, "How come? I was born to farm folks as far back as anyone could remember. But they invited me to a war, and after it was over I figured I'd try something less tedious out this way. I can't say some of it ain't been tedious, but I've seen some sights and made some pals in and out of bed that I might not have if I was cultivating corn on the side of a hill I was born right close to."

She commenced to caress him back as she said, "You're different and I'm so glad already. Most people never stray far from where they were born or take up any new ways of living because, deep inside, they're afraid of new things. Bored out of your mind so you should scream can feel more comfortable than feeling afraid. But confidential, my . . . nerves could use some more soothing, and if you have any new ways we might try . . ."

So he introduced her to dog style, or she said he did. And as he stood there with his bare feet on the braided rug, admiring the view as he gripped a hipbone in either hand to long-dong her at a steady lope, he suddenly had a revelation.

The Indians held that sudden insights into the meaning of it all would come upon a man out of nowhere while he was seated alone on a rock too hungry and thirsty to think along his usual paths of reason. So it seemed possible that mulling over the travails of other peoples in the company of a redhead who bathed regularly had inspired the sudden insight that inspired him to laugh like hell.

"*Nu?* You think my *tush* is to laugh at?" Sadie demanded with her red face buried in the pillows while he fired a salvo into her.

Longarm reached down and around to strum her love-slick banjo as he said soothingly, "I ain't laughing at you, honey. I just had me a sudden thought about that wicked gal who hocked that watch downstairs!"

"You're daydreaming about other women at such a time?" She sobbed, adding, "Just for that, confidential, it's the Baron Rothschild I am having for lunch today! I'm sure he'd be satisfied with a nice Jewish girl and not be mooning over that greasy Roman Catastrophe!"

Then she begged him to stroke her faster and shove it deeper. So he did, and a good time was had by all until once again, damn it to hell, they had to come up for air.

As he lit another smoke, Sadie said, "Before I feed us, what was that *sheis* about your Sister Simone already?"

He explained, "I got to thinking about what you said about most of us going along with the same ways our kith and kin have always followed. Save for the boys down home who got kilt in the war, I was one of the few who pulled up stakes and headed west. You reminded me how lots of folks have trouble shedding old ways no matter how far they roam. Farm folks take up farming. Shop folks open shops, just as if they'd never crossed the main ocean."

She said, "Oy, hold the thought while I get us something to eat. It makes me hungry when I . . . steady my nerves."

So he sat there smoking and sorting his thoughts while Sadie slipped on a kimono and went down to her kitchen to rustle up a late lunch—as it was getting fashionable to call a light dinner. She returned with a tray piled high with cold cuts along with an urn of tea. It was just as well Longarm didn't take sugar and cream with tea because, for some reason, they couldn't have cream at the same meal with kosher salami, and her way of sweetening her own tea was sort of complicated. She served the tea in glasses instead of cups, and held a cube of sugar between her teeth as she drank the tea instead of dropping it in the glass, the way Anglo Americans would have.

But seeing she couldn't talk and sip tea at the same time, Longarm was able to explain, "It came to me at the damnedest time that Sister Simone might have been raised to be a nun whether she wanted to be a nun or not."

"Such things happen?" Sadie asked with difficulty.

He said, "I don't expect the RC Church demands it or *approves* it, for that matter. But say you and mayhaps some other young friends had been raised by old-country kin who sent you to religious schools and whupped you good every time you allowed you'd rather . . . run through a field of sunflowers singing. Say you were forced against your will to take vows as a teaching nun, burning with resentment but with no place to run to until they sent you out west to teach half-wild Indians or free and easy Métis amid wide-open spaces a resentful young gal could get lost in."

Sadie pointed out, "Downstairs she whispered she was

going *back* to that catastrophe, convent, or whatever already."

Longarm said, "I noticed. The Mounties have a picture of her and some other . . . nervous nuns, raising Ned after hours in a back room. So what if Sister Simone never *ran away* from any convent? What if she's been living a double life? What if she's been out raising hell whilst *on leave* from some mission school, convent, or whatever."

"This is allowed?" asked the naked lady having lunch with him.

Longarm said, "I don't know. I have to ask. I do seem to recall some members of religious orders are allowed time off for what they describe as a *sabbatical.* I ain't sure, but I suspect that means a leave of absence like a military furlough. Say she's fairly highly placed as a teaching nun and takes herself off to study, pray, or whatever, but slips off her wimple to let her hair down literally!"

"*Nu?* Enought time she could get away from the other nuns?" the pawnshop owner inquired.

Longarm washed down some salami before he pointed out, "You can hop a train from here to Boston Town or Frisco and back in less than a week, with time to rob a bank in Omaha during a layover there to transfer. They do say she was driving somewhere in a hurry when she was stopped on the border. But what if she did get back a little late this last time, with a good story about lost baggage or poor railroad connections?"

"They wouldn't fuss?" asked Sadie.

He smiled thinly and replied, "They might have. They might not have. How often do you read it in the *Rocky Mountain News* when some soldier on leave or student home for vacation comes back a day or more late? Like I said, I'll have to ask."

"Ask who?" she demurely inquired, pouring another glass of tea.

That was a good question.

He muttered, "Right. It might not be easy getting every mother superior in every convent on this continent to recall which of her sweet-faced charges might have come in a tad late and been allowed to sign in earlier, lest the bishop worry needlessly."

Sadie held her sugar cube in her hand as she sat there cross-legged on the far side of the tray, marveling, "Every convent on this whole continent? Such a lot of places she could be hiding out between her wilder moments?"

Longarm nodded soberly and said, "That's just about the size of it. You heard her tell that gent in the derby she was headed home to her convent two days before yesterday. Say she left Collins that same day, north, south, east, or west, by rail or coach. Can you think of any railroad center, coast to coast north or south of the Canadian border, that she couldn't have made it to by now?"

Sadie sighed and said, "I wish. That means you and your friend won't be staying here in Collins long?"

He answered truthfully, "I don't know. I've already asked and there don't seem to be any nunnery here in this neck of the woods. I ain't sure I'd call Crown Sergeant Foster a friend, but he's not a bad lawman and he's been out scouting for sign as well. We agreed to meet at supper time to compare notes. I just can't say what we might be doing, or where we might be doing it, later on tonight."

She said, "Oy, he hasn't left and already I'm starting to feel . . . nervous again!"

Chapter 7

It hardly seemed possible, but lots of other places were still open for business when he left Sadie's pawnshop. So he headed for the district attorney's office and introduced himself to a mousy little gal with glasses that looked like the bottoms of hotel tumblers. When he said he was interested in the Kramer killing at the pawnshop, she just looked bewildered. But a young squirt who reminded Longarm of Henry, their typewriter player in the Denver office, looked up from his own machine and remarked, "I mind that case, Peg. It was before your time, the summer before last. He's talking about that Jew who got shot by pals of that Frog who got hung for the murder of that Swede. They tried the Frog for killing the Swede in Denver when his lawyers asked for a change in venue. Nobody ever stood trial for killing that Jew. We never found out who done it."

Longarm brightened and declared, "Nobody told me the jasper who'd pawned a dead man's spurs was French! This is commencing to get more interesting and would you care for a cheroot, Mr. . . ."

"Lawrence. Bud Lawrence," the clerk replied, rising from his desk and coming over to the counter barring entrance to the back.

He accepted the cheroot, but put it in a vest pocket for later as he recalled, preening a mite for the mousy Miss Peg, "Gus Persson, a well-to-do stockman, had just sold some beef to the Bureau of Indian Affairs when somebody drygulched him out along the Horsetooth Trail and left him in his long underwear for the carrion crows. They'd robbed him of his money belt and everything else of value including his horse, boots, and saddle. The mistake they made in taking his monogrammed silver-mounted spurs was that Gus had been teased some about them fancy spurs and most everyone around the stockyards had noticed them. So when this dumb Frog, Jacques Cartier, or Jack Carter as some called him around the yards, hocked the selfsame spurs at that Jew place near the yards, he might as well have signed a confession in his own blood."

"You're sure he was French, mayhaps French Canadian, or better yet a Red River Breed?" asked Longarm.

Bud Lawrence shrugged and said, "Could have been anything that works the best for you. Like I said, they tried him for murder down to the capital. So we didn't file much of a brief on him. He said he was French. Said we couldn't hang him because he was an innocent furriner who'd been flimflammed into hocking them spurs by the bad company he'd been keeping. Said he'd won 'em in a card game and never would have hocked them had he known they'd been plucked from a dead man's boots!"

Longarm asked, "I don't suppose anybody considered that he might have been telling the truth?"

The kid who worked for the district attorney shook his head and sounded sure when he replied, "He was lying like a kid caught with a hand in the cookie jar and not a brain in his head. Said he'd fallen in with this gal from his own old country, and that then she'd talked him into a friendly game of cards with these other Frog friends of hers. Have you ever heard of a greenhorn walking into a setup like that and coming out a winner?"

Longarm soberly replied, "Not unless they wanted him to win. Getting a cat's paw to wander about with evidence of a crime on him might have inspired a friendly game of cards indeed. So where's the hole in his story?"

The Fort Collins man snorted in disgust and said, "He made up a mythical hotel near the college to meet this mythical gal and win Gus Persson's spurs in a mythical game of cards. There's no such hotel as he described by any name however sweet anywheres near the college. So what else do you want, an egg in your beer? A man who lied about the way he'd come by them spurs must have known whose spurs they were. He just didn't want to say they were part of his share from the robbery. So he made up a wild tale about being tempted down the primrose path by others he couldn't name in surroundings that don't exist, see?"

Longarm made a wry face and decided, "I liked it better the other way. What if he was confused about the location, being new in Collins and distracted by some lady purring to him in his own lingo? Did he name her, any of the other players, or that hotel near the college at the other end of town?"

Bud Lawrence shrugged and said, "I reckon. But if he named any names up this way, I never took 'em down. Like I said, he was tried for the murderous robbery down in Denver. Not that it did him much good. Old Gus had heaps of pals in these parts, and Denver's only a four-hour train ride. So the prosecution had all the witnesses they needed to convict the lying Frog."

He chuckled and added, "He was still spinning tales about wicked women leading poor boys astray when they sprung the trap under him down Denver way. But if he'd been so innocent, how come his pals shot that pawnbroker for turning Jack Carter in?"

Longarm said he was still working on that. He thanked

the two of them and ambled on to the Western Union near the depot to wire a progress report to Marshal Vail and a request to good old Henry, a file clerk's file clerk. He tersely explained he hardly expected Henry to find anything about a sordid local crime spree in their federal files. But knowing Henry shot pool with other file clerks off Capitol Hill, Longarm asked Henry to see if he could find and forward a transcript of Jacques Cartier's statement to the arresting officers. Asking for transcripts of the whole trial would be asking too much, and would likely make for dull reading besides.

Longarm didn't care whether Cartier had taken part in the robbery or not. He wanted to know whether the poor cuss had named some names, even in a self-serving string of lies. Men talking fast and scared were apt to let things slip.

Crown Sergeant Foster didn't think much of any of Longarm's notions when they met around sunset at the Burlington House.

Seated at the same corner table, with the prim Mountie ordering mashed potatoes and creamed spinach, for Chrissake, with his roast beef, Foster said he'd made arrangements to have Hank Grouleau's body shipped back to Canmont, where he felt honor-bound to be present when they lowered the poor boy's coffin into its prairie grave.

Longarm had ordered chili con carne over a T-bone steak, with extra butter for his sourdough biscuits. As he buttered one, he asked the Mountie if he knew why folks of the Hebrew persuasion were not allowed to have butter on the same table with any kind of meat.

Foster said he had no idea.

Longarm said, "Well, they ain't, and I still say we must be getting warm. That pawnbroker was murdered by pals of a man who might have been a French Canadian. We can surmise other French Canadians pawned that stolen watch at the same shop in the hopes that it would be reported, the same as before. Three of us walked into the trap. They only got one of us. And you figure this would be the time to *leave*?"

Foster tried some of the tea he'd ordered with his own grub, made a wry face, and said, "I have to be there when they bury Grouleau and I very much doubt that, having failed to take either you or me out, our rooftop buffalo hunter has crawled under a wet rock to stay there as long as we have the floor."

Longarm insisted, "If he, she, or it has ducked out of Collins, Canmont can't be the best place to cut their trail again! We cut it down *this* way, damn it!"

Foster pointed out, "You mean they *invited* us here. I say, what on Earth do you Yanks do to tea to make it taste so ghastly?"

Longarm replied in an uncaring tone, "We don't brew tea right, I reckon. But that's only fair. You don't know how to make coffee. I have had decent coffee up Canada way, but it was made American-style by Canadians who like coffee better than tea. You have to like something to know how to prepare it. The worst Chinese food I ever ate was made in Texas by a colored chef, and have you ever tasted an apple pie baked by a Chinaman?"

He stopped with a morsel of steak on the end of his fork and said, "That's twice I've had me a revelation whilst I was concentrating on something less important today. Sister Simone don't know how to dress when she ain't in her nun's habit because, like a Chinaman out to bake an apple pie or an Englishman brewing coffee, she don't know as much about dressing like other gals as other gals do!"

Foster dryly remarked, "I'm sure what you just said made some sense to you. Would you like to try it again, in the Queen's English?"

Longarm said, "Hank Grouleau and them other French-Canadian lawmen thought she looked strange in her own version of Métis costume. Sadie Kramer remarked that she came into their shop in a well-fitting outfit that looked tacky, or just plain *wrong*. Sadie said her hair wasn't right. If she was wearing makeup, she had that wrong as well and it made her look wild and dirty instead of fashionable, as she might have intended. But suppose you'd grown to womanhood in a strict RC convent school and taken vows as a nun before you'd ever read a fashion magazine. Suppose that trying to pass as a . . . civilian, you wound up looking wild and uncivilized instead?"

Foster shrugged and pointed out, "I told you I just can't buy the notion of a disturbed soul leading a double life as a bandit queen and a teaching nun. How would she ever get that much time off? I can see an unhappy nun leaving her nunnery. I can't see her slipping back so she wouldn't be missed between armed robberies!"

Longarm swallowed that morsel, sipped some coffee, and replied, "Not an *enlisted* nun. But what if she'd two-faced her way up the chain of command, just carrying on dirty on the premises until she saw her way clear to write her *own* furloughs? The gent who first said rank had its privileges knew what he was about. Let me tell you a tale about the late George Armstrong Custer and his pretty young wife, Miss Libby. He was finally found out, and almost lost his commission, after he'd overdone his stolen moments with his lady love a mite. I suspect he was only reported absent from his post a lot because a lot of other officers hated him pure and simple. Had he been a regular feller around the offices' club, he'd have doubtless been home in bed with his Libby whilst Crazy Horse scalped Reno or Benteen. So what if Sister Simone is a popular nun of some stature and—"

"My God, the next thing you'll accuse her of is the position of mother superior!"

"The thought never crossed my mind," Longarm lied.

Foster said, "Wasn't it you who warned us about sniffing and woofing in wild circles? Frankly, all this sniffing and woofing about local killings and unfashionable ladies' wear seems to be leading us nowhere, and I have to catch the northbound night train out of Denver. They've offered to load poor Grouleau's coffin aboard the baggage car for us, but they expect me to get on myself."

Longarm muttered, half under his breath, "Shit, if I'd known Her Majesty's Government wasn't all that interested, I'd have stayed on the case I was working in the high country. There was this mapping gal I'd just got to know and . . . Never mind. I have to stay put here for now, seeing I've sent to Denver for some transcripts, and what the hell, I might look up some other folks I know here in Collins."

It was none of Her Majesty's business whether the smoldering Widow Sloan or the frisky Widow Kramer still liked him.

They finished their grub, and Longarm was a sport about helping the Mountie in mufti get his own shit over to the depot in the gathering dusk. As they stood there waiting for the train up from Denver, Longarm was just as glad he'd left his own possibles at the hotel. The night ride north was tempting, as far as Cheyenne. But he couldn't see much point in riding on to the Canadian line, and he knew almost as many gals who put out in Collins as he could count on in Cheyenne.

The railroad ran alongside the Cache la Poudre through the northeast corner of town. So street lamps illuminated one side of the long open platform, with the cricket-haunted darkness of the yard sidings and floodplain to the northeast.

They'd only stood there a spell with Foster's baggage when the rubber-rimmed hearse from the undertaker's rolled in and four husky hands unloaded Hank Grouleau's crated coffin. As they placed it where the baggage car figured to stop alongside the platform, Longarm and

61

Foster toted the Mountie's possibles up that way, then shook all around and lit up some smokes.

They had less than a quarter hour to kill that way before the northbound's locomotive chased its headlamp beam up the track past them, clanging fit to bust as it slowed to a stop.

They saw they were in the right place when the side door of that baggage car looming above them slid open. They naturally had to wait while the railroaders unloaded some shit destined for Collins. You let freight and passengers off before you invited either to board.

But it didn't take long, seeing only a few passengers, their checked-through baggage, and some mail-order crates with a couple of mailbags had to get past them.

Then Longarm and the burly Mountie helped the others lift Grouleau's crate and shove it over the steel sill along the plank floor of the baggage car.

The engine's brass bell started to clang some more. So Longarm and Foster were shaking adios near the boarding steps of the baggage car when a six-gun cleared its throat for attention, down alongside another car, and both lawman spun away from each other, slapping leather as they spun.

Longarm landed in a gunfighter's crouch with his .44–40 trained on a slender dark outline surrounded by thinning gun smoke. But he didn't fire because he could see another figure sprawled on the platform way closer and the tableau only read one way.

"Advance and be recognized, friend," called Longarm. More for the ears of the nearby Foster, lest he fire in haste.

The mysterious figure who'd just backshot somebody else instead of either lawman moved forward into a puddle of lamplight, a .38 Colt Detective held politely. He turned into a pale, thin drink of water who usually played the typewriter back at Longarm's home office.

So Longarm called out, "Well, howdy, Henry. I didn't think you had it in you!"

To which the wide-eyed Henry could only reply, "Neither did I. Would you like to tell me who I just shot?"

Longarm moved that way, asking, "Don't you know him, Henry?"

The clerk and typist soberly replied, "There wasn't time for formal introductions. He had that buffalo gun trained on you or that other gentleman pointing his gun at me."

Chapter 8

Foster put his own .455 back in its shoulder holster to join the growing crowd around the body oozing into the sun-silvered planks of the loading platform.

The buffalo gun Henry had mentioned lay on the ballast between the platform's edge and the steel rails occupied by the northbound at the moment.

When Longarm held it up to the light, he could see it had been meant as an *elephant* gun by its maker, Parker of London. It was a breech-loading double-barrel rifle chambered for awesome .51–250 rounds that would stop far more than your average buffalo.

The derby hat had rolled off the platform into the weeds between the planking and the cinder-paved street. When they rolled the dead man over, they saw he was a pasty-faced dumpy cuss who looked to have been fashioned out of sourdough. His wallet held thirty-eight paper dollars and a Denver library card made out to one Jules Chambrun. Longarm read a lot for a country boy. So he knew how easy it was to get a library card just by filling out a slip, and that Chambrun had been the family name of the Marquis de Lafayette.

When Longarm and Foster agreed the dead man fit the description given by the Widow Kramer, a nearby copper badge volunteered to fetch her over to the morgue.

Longarm and Foster, along with Henry, of course, stayed with the body as it waited there for the coroner's dray.

Henry explained that Marshal Vail, seeing that Western Union charged a scandalous nickel a word and they had plenty of courtesy passes from the railroad line, had ordered Henry to just run those transcripts up to Longarm in person that evening.

As he handed a bulky hemp-paper envelope over, Henry naturally wanted to know why.

Suddenly Foster let fly a curse, started running, and gave up with a display of foot-stamping resignation as the train rolled off into the night.

Longarm calmly explained, "We just loaded another Henry, spelled with an I, aboard yonder train in his coffin. I reckon we'll have to wire he'll be arriving alone."

Henry said, "I read the wires you sent us earlier today. That's my job. I read the statement the late Jacques Cartier gave when he was arrested for the murder of one Gustav Persson. I didn't see anything but confused self-tripping twaddle about people and places the Fort Collins lawmen had never heard of."

Longarm put the envelope away, saying he had to read it before he'd know whether he'd wasted his time or not. Within minutes they had the modestly self-described Jules Chambrun on his way to the morgue and a pro forma autopsy, or quick medical exam. Nobody had the least doubt about the cause of death. Henry said he'd be proud to dictate a deposition for them.

So that was about what was going on when they brought Sadie Kramer into the basement autopsy theater. The Widow Kramer took one look at the face of the hastily covered cadaver and exclaimed, "Oy, it's him! The one who pawned that stolen watch with the nunnery woman who should bathe more often!"

Foster said that made no sense. Longarm agreed with

him, and allowed he'd run the unsettled Widow Kramer home while the proceedings at the morgue went on.

He did. So after some quick loving to settle her nerves, he got back as they were sewing the dumpy corpse back together with butcher's twine. The Fort Collins deputy coroner dryly said, "Caliber-.38 lodged in the sternum after passing through the aorta over the heart, as I'd assumed from all that postmortem bleeding. Who's going to take this stiff off our hands now that we've no further use for it?"

Longarm directed Henry to handle that paperwork as well, seeing it had been his grand notion to kill the gent.

Telling Henry to meet them in the taproom of the Burlington House, Longarm explained the draconian rules of the U.S. Justice Department to the Mountie as they legged it the short way back to their hotel.

To discourage needless shootouts, the regulations governing a federal lawman's duties saddled the lawman who killed an outlaw with the disposal of the corpse.

A lot of times a dead outlaw's kith and kin came forward to claim the body, and by traditions going back to Roman law, a dead criminal, having paid his debts to the state, became a part of his own estate and thus the private property of his heirs.

Seeing that he was explaining this to one of Her Britannic Majesty's lawmen, Longarm couldn't resist adding, "That bullshit about heads on poles above London Bridge or Captain Kidd's remains being dipped in tar and hung in chains as an example to other pirates would have struck them Romans who crucified Our Lord as barbaric. The Good Book says them pagan Romans handed His dead flesh over to His kith and kin for proper burial, once they'd finished torturing Him to death."

"We don't intend to draw and quarter Sister Simone when we catch her," Foster snorted. "Then your office is stuck with that possible British subject, unless nobody comes forward?"

Longarm said, "That's about the size of it. But look on the bright side. You'd be surprised how often a not-too-bright crook strides right into our welcoming arms, asking about the remains of a pal as ought to be sent home to his poor old momma. Marshal Vail gets reduced rates from this undertaking firm in Denver, unless you'd rather haul the dead cuss back to Canada. It's your right. We ain't barbarians."

Under a hanging lantern above a table in the taproom at the hotel, Longarm opened the envelope and spread its onionskin contents on the maple tabletop to peruse while Foster ordered a pitcher of suds and composed his long wire to Fort MacLeod, explaining about the body aboard the train.

Jacques Cartier, or Jack Carter as he'd preferred to be known south of the border, hadn't used up all that many pages trying to explain a lot that nobody else had bought.

His simple story of an honest young cowboy falling in with bad company held together fairly well, until you got to a hotel that wasn't over by the college campus or anywhere else in Fort Collins, according to some postscript after Cartier's signature.

Henry came in to join them, flopping down to exclaim, "There. That's over, and now how in the world am I supposed to get back to Denver this evening?"

Foster said he'd heard the Fort Collins red-light district, south of Prospect Road, ran wide open night and day. Foster didn't know Henry as well as Longarm, who suspected the pallid youth was working his way up to jacking off.

Longarm told Henry there was a southbound combination passing through this side of midnight, and added, "We'll have you back in your crib before cock's crow, Henry, and how often do I have to tell you they don't pay you one cent extra for getting to the office as early as you and the boss? Old Billy won't be expecting you to beat him to work. He reads the railroad timetables.

You could likely get away with reporting in after dinner break."

Henry looked as if Longarm had proposed he make mad Gypsy love to his own mother, but accepted a stein of beer and some petrified wood fashioned in• the shape of pretzels.

Foster looked up from his own scribbling to declare, "They'll get this in plenty of time to have an honor guard waiting when poor Hank Grouleau arrives properly packaged. When might I board the next train north? I know I'll never catch up with Grouleau's coffin in time, but I have to try."

Longarm asked mildy, "How come? Hank's dead as a turd in a milk bucket, and Henry here just nailed one of the gang you're after here in Colorado."

Foster shoved his papers aside and consumed some lager as he thought about that, then decided, "I can't make it work. That dumpy lad with the Parker .51–250 and derby with a Montreal label as much as invited us here to ambush us, only got one of us, and—"

"Tried some more." Longarm nodded. "I suspect they were out to establish Fort Collins as the town where they met up with Jack Carter. I reckon they banked on him needing some eating money by the time he got here to Fort Collins. He told the arresting officers he'd been sort of drifting along the Front Range, looking for work at the cattle spreads along the Front Range."

Longarm sipped some suds to wet his own whistle and continued. "They could have hung the wrong man. That part of his story works. Most of the stock spreads along the foothill trail are modest one-family operations and he'd started late for the fall roundup. All the extra help as might have been needed could have already been hired."

"Then what was he doing in a game of high-stakes poker?" asked Henry, who'd said he'd copied the transcript from court records.

Longarm said, "He swore he'd only been looking for romance when his path crossed that of a lady who said, in French, he could call her Yvette. It was her notion they go to her hotel, and he says he didn't want to play cards with some other Canadians there until he suddenly got to winning. He says that after the game he split his winnings with the lady known as Yvette, described as black-haired and sort of Gypsy-looking if you follow my drift."

Foster shrugged and said, "Well, of course that sounds like Sister Simone, without her wimple and rosary, but that was obviously just a slip. He described a female member of his gang when someone asked him by surprise what this mythical Yvette looked like."

"He made a lot of other stuff up from thin air," Henry agreed.

Longarm sighed and said, "I'm afraid he might not have. I'm afraid the State of Colorado could owe his kith and kin an apology along with such damages as they'll settle for. He could've been used as a dupe by Sister Simone, who, as his lady of the evening named Yvette, got most of his ready cash and sold him the notion he could get a good deal on the spurs he'd won if he went to a pawnbroker she knew here in Collins."

"Lady of the evening?" marveled Henry, who didn't get out much.

"She took him to bed and screwed him dizzy," said Longarm without hesitation. "I know it don't say so in his statement, Henry. The poor wayfaring stranger was trying to be delicate. He never says right out he was framed by a gal he'd thought he was screwing with."

"That's not saying she . . . went all the way with him," Henry almost pleaded. Longarm sometimes got the notion Henry didn't want anybody to have any fun.

Longarm swilled more suds, repressed a belch, and said, "Trust me on this, gents. The only way it works is that she screwed him, kept him screwed, blued, and confused as she got him on and off a local train into a fleabag near the Collins stockyards, and left him there flat broke and slowly coming to his senses. Wandering about to get his bearings, he spied the three gold balls of the very pawnshop his Yvette had suggested. So he went on over, hocked a dead man's spurs, and found himself in deep shit, trying to explain his way out of it. From some of the stilted wording of this transcript, he must have had a hell of an accent they had to guess some about. So he might have been a confused traveler or something might have been missed in translation. But suffice it to say, nobody believed him and he was found guilty on circumstantial evidence. After a short trial and a hasty public hanging, other members of the gang went back to murder the pawnbroker, Morris Kramer. He might or might not have remembered things their dead dupe might or might not have said when he was hocking them spurs, see?"

Crown Sergeant Foster exclaimed, "I don't see at all. Are you trying to imply this mysterious meeting with a mysterious French-speaking *femme fatale* took place in *another town*?"

Longarm said, "I ain't implying it. Jack Carter says right here on page two that Miss Yvette invited him to her quarters at the Flatiron Hotel near the college campus, where they met up with a whole bunch of other fictitious names."

He let that sink in and explained. "I doubt anybody would name a hotel after a household item. The flatirons—there are three of 'em—are these bodacious slabs of red sandstone rising southwest of the town of *Boulder,* not Fort Collins, a few rail stops south. I really don't know what tilted them big slabs the color of rusty iron skyward and eroded them to look like the rounded points of flatirons, but it did, and there they stand, dominating the view to the west with all sorts of saloons, drugstores, and of course a hotel named after them!"

Henry protested, "But the accused insisted he'd met

his Yvette as the two of them were strolling on the college campus in the gloaming and spent some time there on a bench before she invited him to her Flatiron Hotel across the way so . . . Oh, good heavens, of course!"

Foster said he was starting to feel left out, and demanded to know what they were talking about.

Longarm explained, "The college campus here in Fort Collins goes with Colorado Agricultural College. Poor Carter only remembered the Colorado part, and of course the law here in Fort Collins assumed that was the Colorado College he was jawing about, excited and half in French."

"There's another Colorado College?" asked the Canadian.

Longarm nodded grimly and said, "More like the Boulder campus of the University of Colorado, founded five years after Colorado Agriculture and dismissed as an upstart that only opened full time in the fall of '77. But it's still there, just a few stops away, with a campus to meet false-hearted women whilst roaming in the gloaming as a stranger in these parts!"

Foster gasped, "I say, that may well mean they wanted us here in Fort Collins dead because they never wanted us to take them dead or alive down in Boulder!"

Longarm said, "That works for me." He turned to Henry to tell the clerk and typist, "I want you to wait here for that later train. When you get into Denver, tell old Billy I'll wire from Boulder if and when I learn more than you can tell him."

Henry looked confused, and asked, "Aren't you going to board the same train with me? It's only the third stop down the line."

Longarm replied, "I can't speak for the sarge here, but I mean to hire a livery mount for some night riding. It's way slower, but may be surer than getting off a train where some other son of a bitch with a high-powered

71

rifle could be watching from many a window!"

Crown Sergeant Foster patted the bulge under his frock coat and said, "You just spoke well enough for me, Yank."

Chapter 9

A man got to really appreciate the wonders of modern transportation when riding one pony and leading a spare through the night. For while the train would have dropped them off in Boulder within three hours, they were fixing to spend two days in the saddle with layovers in Loveland and Lyons for a few winks and fresh ponies, if they made good times and the creeks didn't rise. Trail towns had sprung up an average day's ride apart with just such riding in mind. So Henry would be at the office in Denver before they were a third of the way down to Boulder. But Foster agreed it might be best to show up unexpectedly for a change.

During the twenty-odd-mile night ride to Loveland, not daring to run strange mounts along unfamiliar trails in the dark, Longarm got to know Crown Sergeant Foster better than he'd ever wanted to. Brought to Canada as a kid by his folks, his father being a clerk with the Hudson Bay Company, Foster had been born in England, spent time there as a schoolboy, and didn't want anyone to ever forget that. He allowed as he'd rowed for Harrow, and would have gone on to explain if Longarm hadn't told him he'd read about those college boys holding rowboat races on the River Thames. When he added he'd read the boys from Eton usually won, Foster said that was an astounding fabrication.

Not wanting to argue about boat racing or his own more modest school days, Longarm explained what made the Rocky Mountains so rocky.

Folks who'd never seen them pictured the Rockies as they looked on many a postcard, strung along the horizon as a jagged-ass sawtooth of snowcapped peaks. Down Denver way, tourists were always heading over to the seemingly near Front Range on foot, convinced that they rose just on the edge of town and that they were the main range of those famous Rocky Mountains.

The Front Range only commenced to rise seriously around fifteen miles or a five-hour ride west of Denver. Horses averaged no more than three miles an hour walking up even a gentle grade.

After you got to the foothills you couldn't see from Denver, and commenced to suspect there might be more to the Rocky Mountains than appeared from a hotel window in town, you were only in the Front Range if you climbed to the peaky tops. From Lookout Mountain, just west of Golden, you could see across Denver into the hazy horizons of the High Plains, and then stroll around to stare off into the west at even higher peaks. For there really was no main range of the Rockies.

Even the dotted line on the maps that showed the official Continental Divide was based more on the way mountain creeks drained than how high or low the land really rose. The old Overland Trail and modern TransContinental railroad crossed the Continental Divide over wide-open rolling prairie with nothing to indicate the waters flowing east and west. Other passes over the Divide were so high and steep, it was a wonder anyone had ever found them. Like the big fault-block of the Front Range, a whole lot of others, each a mighty mountain range in its own right, ran more or less the same directions as the ox-bowed dotted map line of the Divide, unless they ran some other way for a piece.

Taking breaks and changing mounts once an hour, Longarm and Foster made fair time. They passed lonely points of lamplight, and got barked at some by distant dogs until ten or so. A tad after midnight that southbound combination with Henry on board tore down the tracks, off to their east, laughing at them fit to bust with its puffing diamond-stack.

Foster swore softly and said, "I think I see why that other poor Canadian lad was confused as to just where he was. When one's used to getting about on horseback, this world seems a lot bigger, doesn't it!"

Longarm replied, "Hauled aboard a train half likkered-up by a soft and friendly female, a man could think he'd only rid a hop, skip, and jump. We'll have to ask Sister Simone about that when we catch her. I fear it's a tad late to ask the late Jack Carter."

Longarm felt no call to argue when Foster said using a fellow Canuck like that had been nastier than necessary. But Foster still went on. "They'd killed that rich Swede and gotten away clean. They could have simply chucked those spurs where nobody would have found them. It was needlessly vicious to frame that poor drifter Sister Simone seems to have stumbled over by chance!"

Longarm said, "Well, a convent gal who poses for the camera with a wine bottle up her twat might just *enjoy* being vicious. You can butcher a cow without blowing bugles and parading around in gold braid. They butcher cows all day in a slaughterhouse without that much drama. But heaps of otherwise pleasant folks just enjoy such noise and excitement. Maybe going to bed with a gent you're planning to set up for a frame is exciting to some gals. I've heard men brag about the bullshit they were handing some poor trusting spinster they were screwing. It's not as easy to feel clever as all get-out jacking off."

Foster asked, "Do you think something as sick as that

75

is driving Sister Simone? If, as you suggest, she's found a safe and comfortable niche with her church, as a two-faced trusted nun of some stature, she must feel so clever about fooling us all that she may not need a man, or a bottle, to pleasure her nasty soul!"

Longarm didn't want to brag. So he didn't go into the many cases of sheer evil for the sake of evil he'd cracked in his six or eight years with the Justice Department. He just said, "Some crazy folks do sort of remind one of wolverines. I reckon you'd have to be a wolverine instead of just a hungry bear or shit-eating dog to understand why wolverines tear up a camp or cabin so spitefully. What a wolverine can't eat or fuck, it's inclined to tear apart and shower with liquid shit. Sister Simone seems to include things she fucks. I'll bet that after she posed with that wine bottle, she busted it and crapped on the shattered glass. That might be a weakness we can use against her. If only I ever cut her infernal trail."

Before Foster could object, Longarm added, "I mean her *real* trail. Not a trail she's *left* for us, like bread crumbs leading under some propped-up box-trap."

They rode into Loveland by cock's crow and Longarm, knowing the place better, took the lead.

Loveland was named for an earlier rider named Love. It wasn't all that lovely. It was just a bitty trail town where folks off the surrounding spreads could shop and pick up their mail. As the dawn light painted the peaks to the west pink, Longarm bet the hostlers at the one livery that he and Foster couldn't swap for fresh riding stock and spread their bedrolls in the loft for a four-hour nap for two bucks. After they'd lost and been sent on their way before nine by the gleeful stable hands, they got to ride faster by daylight.

Taking breaks and swapping ponies as before, they rode along the grassy eastern flanks of the Front Range with the longspurs atwitter and the short grass, mostly buffalo, bunch, and grama, still fairly green. The ponies, being Colorado stock, didn't shy as some might have at those big prairie grasshoppers, disguised as lumps of 'dobe until they exploded out from under you, buzzing their black and yellow butterfly wings like rattlesnakes, to land and disappear some more down the road ahead, until you got close enough for them to repeat their performance.

The older trail, winding more than the rails to the east, crested gentle grass-grown groundswells to dip down across riparian corridors, as the government survey men called the more verdant wooded draws that wound out across the High Plains from the foothills.

Tall cottonwoods, a sort of poplar, grew cheek by jowel with box elder, a sort of maple, with tanglewoods of chokecherry, crack willow, and such feeding mountain critters well out across the plains in some cases. The railroad crossed such draws on trestles. Folks riding or driving the trail got to ford fetlock-deep in some draws, stirrup-deep in others. When Foster bitched about wet boots, Longarm told him they'd missed the serious spring thaws.

They flushed lots of grouse and jackrabbits while riding along, and one startled mule deer browsing cottonwood sprouts. But they mostly spooked cows, black Cherokee and calico Texas beef stock shading in the draws as the sun rose higher.

They passed a home spread every mile or less, set on higher ground where the winter winds blew crueler but the unpredictable floods couldn't get at you.

They naturally got coffee'd and caked half a dozen times before they rode into Lyons around sundown. So neither was all that hungry as they made another horse swap and decided to sleep until midnight.

There was more to their method than trail weariness. There was a telegraph office in Lyons, a somewhat larger trail town than Loveland, drawing a bigger crowd of an evening. So they figured it would be best to ride on after

Lyons simmered down for the night, when they'd notice anybody paying a hell of a lot of attention to them.

The rest of the night slowly passed as they made sure and steady progress. By the time they rode into Boulder, they were more convinced than ever that a drifting cowhand, making it up to Collins within a few hours, could easily believe he was only a short ways from that "Colorado College" others kept fussing at him about. Although in point of fact, Boulder and the University of Colorado were an easy day's ride out of Denver in the saddle and less than an hour by rail.

Gold seekers had horned in on the Arapaho camped in the foothills around the mouths of Boulder and El Dorado Canyons back around the time others struck color in Cherry Creek, as Denver was called to begin with, just before the Civil War. El Dorado Canyon had led to no such place. But Boulder Canyon offered a watered route west through the Front Range to the wide grassy "parks" and gold fields higher in the Rockies. As in the case of Fort Collins, the downtown business district of Boulder lay north of the college campus, although the street grid was laid out a bit different, with streets running north and south having numbers, while streets running east and west rated names. Pearl Street, running east and west north of the brawling Boulder Creek that roared through town between the business district and the University Hill district around the campus, was the main drag of Boulder. Everything from the courthouse and imposing Arnett-Fullen Mansion to rotgut saloons and the municipal corral was strung out along Pearl Street. So they'd timed it to ride along Pearl Street around quitting time, when two more riders on a crowded street would be less likely to attract attention.

By the same logic, the two lawmen split up at the municipal corral. As Longarm bartered with the hostlers about their ponies and a place to store their saddles and possibles, Foster went to send some wires and attend to some shopping they'd agreed upon.

A society run on steam and horsepower had fairly uniform conventions about horseflesh. Horse theft was punishable by death in the state of Colorado, not because horses were stolen that often, but lest horses be stolen at all. Leaving a fellowman stranded on foot could leave him in mortal danger on occasion.

On other occasions you could buy an unbroken scrub pony for less than ten dollars and hire a fair livery mount for two bits a day plus deposit. Livery stables and corrals throughout the West in most every trail town, river crossing, and such were independently owned for the most part, but most often perforce in cahoots with one another along well-traveled trails.

A rider traveling far with his own mount, which happened when the pony was a prized possession, took his time and stopped over a lot, with his pet pony cared for overnight at each livery along the way. A rider in more of a hurry hired a nag at one livery, rode it to the next, and swapped it, forfeiting his first deposit but using the jaded mount as deposit on the next, and riding on to repeat the procedure as far as he needed to go. When he got there, he could usually get his forfeit money back in exchange for the pony he rode in on. The fun came from the wheeling and dealing each time you swapped. But livery nags were livery nags, usually over-the-hill cow ponies, so it averaged out. The livery owners always came out ahead. They broke even on the swaps, and put away that extra two bits a head per day. Because they kept in touch, it was tough to get away with hiring a pony for one day and riding it for two. They'd know how far and how long you'd ridden a mount you aimed to swap, and haggled accordingly, sharing profits up and down the trail the way stockmen grazing the same range settled up at roundup time.

The last four ponies Longarm and Foster dismounted

from in Boulder had been fair livery stock, however long in the tooth. A cow pony too old to cut and rope with was far from a doddering cripple. A three- or four-year-old remuda bronc lived the life, and had to be in the shape of a human athlete. A six- or eight-year-old livery nag of the cow pony persuasion could still give a man a ride for his money.

So Longarm dickered the livery in Boulder down to a fair settlement and rejoined Foster, as planned, at the municipal bathhouse.

Like livery stables, public baths offering plenty of hot water and a little privacy were a profitable necessity, and would continue to be until such time as far more working folks could afford indoor plumbing.

Public baths were used for more than public bathing. So the colored attendant just smirked when Longarm and the burly Mountie said they wanted to share a private steam chamber and dressing room.

But they kept their hands to themselves as they stripped, got rid of some trail dust, and put on the new outfits Foster had bought for them. Knowing anybody expecting them in Boulder would picture them in their now-dusty dark suits, they left the municipal bathhouse in summer suits of pinstriped seersucker. New denim stood out until it had been washed a lot, and seemed informal for a strange hotel, so they left their duds at a tailor shop on north-south Broadway. Then they headed down the street, toting only their saddlebags, with all their other shit in the livery's tack room.

They crossed Boulder Creek and, sure enough, a four-story hotel that called itself after those flatirons to the west stood between the tree-lined creek and the college campus to the south.

They went on in and hired adjoining rooms on the top floor without incident. The desk clerk rang up a dusky young gal in gathered skirts and a bell boy jacket to show them the way up the three flights of stairs. Longarm noticed Foster only tipped her a dime as she put his key in the lock and opened his door for him. So when she led Longarm on to the room next door, he thanked her, commented on all those stairs, and tipped her a quarter.

She stared down at the handsome reward in her palm without visible emotion. Her hair was parted, and braided full-blood as well. When she did look up, her eyes were glistening. She glanced about, nodded, and told him, "I know who you must be. You are the one my people call Wasichu Wastey, and I know why you have come here. You are after that *weyhah witco* of the Arapaho Nation. I am Martha Was-Yellow. I am a Christian. How may I help you?"

Chapter 10

Some things she'd just said were clear to Longarm as he shut the hall door behind her and tossed his saddlebags on the bedstead. If her elders called him Wasichu Wastey, or "Good White Man" if you aimed to translate it politely, she had to be Lakota, sort of. Adopting that family name of Was-Yellow, now that the Interior Department required wards of the government to settle on family names and stick to them, sounded as if someone a ways back might have been Cheyenne. Cheyenne were forever naming things yellow because it was a brave medicine color. After that, things weren't as clear.

Had Denver been named after local Indians, the way Cheyenne to the north had, instead of after a former governor of a Greater Kansas that had extended to the Continental Divide, Denver would have been called Arapaho. For in their Shining Times, the small but truculent Arapaho Nation had held the foothills and High Plains between the North Platte and Arkansas Rivers against all comers. Arapaho warriors had invented the suicidal display of valor known as "Singing to the Stake." Their Red Sash Lodge wore long sashes of crimson trade cloth to make this battle tactic easier. An Arapaho electing to cover the retreat of his band or a horse-stealing expedition would unravel a few yards of his long sash and stake one end of it to the sod with the other end still wrapped around his middle. Then he'd just stay put, singing his death song with his bow in one hand, a war club in the other, and as many arrows as he had handy driven into the sod in front of him. One of the finest brags any warrior of another nation could sing about at a scalp dance was that he'd charged in on a stake-singing Arapaho, to slap him on the head without drawing blood, and scampered out of range again, laughing at the poor excited cuss.

More pragmatic enemies, and just about all white men, had found it simpler to just pick a stake-singer off from a safe distance, and that had likely been the reason there had been so few Arapaho left to take part in the serious Indian fighting after the War Between the States. Under pressure from Wagons West, the Arapaho had merged with their Cheyenne cousins to be the less famous if no less ferocious Horse Indians. Driven deeper into the Rockies, the Arapaho had done as much as or more than the Colorado Volunteers to push the Mountain Ute clean out to Utah Territory.

But Longarm hadn't been sent to Boulder after any Arapaho, male or female, so he asked the Lakota gal what they might be talking about.

Martha Was-Yellow said, "They did not know I understood what they were talking about. That one woman they were sharing asked me, when they arrived, what nation I was from. She seemed pleased when I told her I was a Christian Lakota. The Lakota tongue is nothing like that of the Arapaho, Cheyenne, or our ancient enemies, the Ojibwa by the vast Minnetonka. I had no reason to tell her my grandmother had been born a Cheyenne, or that I had been named after her. So later, when I heard them snickering about me among themselves in their own tongue, I pretended I did not understand anything they said."

She looked as pissed as most full-bloods allowed themselves to look as she added, "I did not understand every word. I should have paid more attention when my grandmother tried to teach her old ways to us. But I understand enough Cheyenne, *good* Cheyenne, to know they were not speaking good Cheyenne. Many words were the same, but spoken in a funny way. Other words were new to me. But when a man grins at you and says he thinks you would like it in a silly position, you do not have to know every word."

Longarm started to reach for some money, thought better of it, and got out a cheroot as he confided, "That other lawman and me are after four or five men and a wild-looking woman who might be Canadian Métis or Red River Breeds. They'd have no call to speak Arapaho or Cheyenne. But Plains Cree is a dialect related to both, and how long can you stay up here without getting in trouble?"

She allowed it might be best if they waited until she got off duty. When she added that her regular quitting time was sundown, Longarm glanced out the nearby window at the flatirons rising blackly against the late afternoon sun and lit the cheroot. Then he soberly told her, "I will be waiting. We have a heap to talk about." Then he placed the lit cheroot to her lips. She crawfished back and stammered, "Wasichu Wastey offers to *smoke* with me, a *woman*?"

Longarm soberly replied, "Brave hearts who hunt together should smoke together. I have to tell you, Miss Martha, the people we are hunting are more dangerous than staked-out Arapaho or the riders of your own Contrary Lodge. They're as ready to kill, but they kill like cowards. Clever cowards. I want you to think about that as you head back downstairs. If you don't want to risk your very life in a fight that ain't your own, don't come back and we'll say no more about it."

The assimilated full-blood reached up to take the cheroot from his hand, help herself to a deep drag on it, and blow smoke up, down, and sideways before she handed the cheroot back, softly saying, "I will be back before dark!"

When she'd left, Foster rapped on the door and let himself in to asked, "What was all that about? I could hear the two of you muttering in here, but I couldn't make out what you were saying. Are you out to change your luck with a little squaw-banging?"

Longarm said, "She ain't a squaw, she's a *weyah*. Sister Simone seems to be the squaw, or *esquaw* as most Algonquin-speakers really say it."

He repeated what Martha Was-Yellow had just told him. Foster said, "We already knew Sister Simone speaks some Cree. Let's not get carried away. A teaching nun as white as the driven snow, or, all right, an Irish Gypsy of the same qualifications, might know enough Cree to get by. This other Indian wench wouldn't have known whether they were making lewd remarks about her in fluent or crude Trader's Cree, eh, what?"

Longarm replied simply, "I don't know. I mean to question her some more about that if she comes back. If she does come back, she might feel more like talking if just the two of us . . ."

Foster cut in. "I was meaning to go roaming in the gloaming on the college campus to the south in any case. Is the University of Colorado coeducational?"

Longarm said he doubted any state college was ready for that much progress. So the Canadian said, "Pity. But if that other lad found the greens of UC a happy hunting ground, I may be able to meet some young friends who can fill me in on the local rules of engagement."

Longarm started to make a sassy observation about dirty old mounted policemen. But on reflection, Foster's notion made sense. The way of a man with a maid did vary some as one wandered a vast horny world. The way you picked up a *señorita* at a Mexican *paseo* was nothing like the way things went at a Sunday-Go-to-Meeting-on-the-Green or the Oktoberfest at Kellerman's Beer Garden. If Jack Carter had really picked up Sister Simone on the nearby campus grounds, she might or might not have been following some local customs. And they weren't fixing to learn them without asking about them.

So they shook on it and Foster left, with his .455 concealed under his loose seersucker jacket.

It seemed to take a million years for that infernal sun to get on down.

He took advantage of the time on his hands to tidy some. He hung his Stetson and new seersucker jacket on wall hooks, and draped his two saddlebags over the brass rail at the foot of the bedstead. He left his holstered .44–40 and the vest-pocket derringer in his seersucker vest until he felt surer of his surroundings. He was worried about the saddle gun he'd left in the tack room at the livery. But they'd assured him the livery hadn't been robbed in recent memory, and a stranger trying to blend in where he might be expected to show up had no call to stride down the streets with a Winchester '73.

They'd been amused downstairs when he and Foster had asked about rooms with baths. But though there was no commode or hot water and you had to go down the hall for either, they had put a wet-sink with a cold-water tap in a corner. So although he knew it was a nasty habit, Longarm took a good leak in the sink, rinsed the head of his old organ-grinder, and ran the tap wide open to wash his sins away, not wanting to be different from any of the other gents who'd ever hired that room.

The Front Range rose black as India ink against a western sky the color of sliced smoked salmon by the time he heard a hesitant tap on the door and opened it to let Martha Was-Yellow in. The little Lakota had changed to a blue polka-dot Mother Hubbard, and painted the part of her hair vermillion. That made as much sense as cheek rouge applied over a good sun-tan, which many a farm

gal did when she was aiming for something more allur-
ing.

Longarm was more interested in the willow hamper
Martha was carrying, along with a folded red and black
trade blanket. He'd almost forgotten in the excitement of
the last few hours that neither he nor Foster had eaten
since that coffee and cake stop around three that afternoon. So he hoped he was smelling what he hoped he
was smelling, and when she set the hamper on the bed
and lifted its willow lid, he had been.

She'd brought half a loaf of sliced rye bread along with
jars of butter and mustard, cold cuts from sliced ham to
salami, a wedge of cheese, and lest that not be enough,
a quart jar of potato salad. To wash it all down, she'd
provided a jug of hard cider. Since she worked there,
Martha had known about the thick glass tumblers that
came with the sink, Turkish towel, and free cakes of
soap. But she'd borrowed napkins and dining room sil-
verware while she'd been at it. So Longarm proceeded
to build them a couple of heroic sandwiches as she carefully spread her blanket atop the hotel's braided rug.

Carefully because, as was the custom of her nation, the
four corners of the rug had to point at the four cardinals
of north, south, east, and west no matter how the Wasichu
had laid out a whole hotel in total disregard of the Wakan
Tonka, or Great Medicine, which was closer to what they
meant than that Great Spirit popularized by white poets.

Not having the disadvantage of a written-down dogma
they had to stick with, the shirt-wearers or important elders white men described as medicine men felt more responsible for their revelations, and tended to admit it
when they simply didn't know. Horse Indians of all the
Plains Nations knew what had happened to poor old
Kicking Bird, the Comanche medicine man who'd advised that disasterous attack at Adobe Wells. So, de-
pending on who you asked, Wakan Tonka was Great
Medicine or indescribable power/luck, a Great Mystery

that just *was,* or sometimes a giver of laws and traditions closer to the white man's notion of a Great Spirit. The one thing they all agreed on was that it was a dangerous notion to go against the few known rules of Wakan Tonka, and one of them was that the Wasichu built everything all wrong, at a forty-five-degree angle to the way they should have.

Having spread her red-and-black-striped blanket according to her own notions of Wakan Wastey or *Good* Medicine, the Lakota who claimed to be a Christian rose to face him, eyes shyly lowered to his seated crotch.

When Longarm held out a ham, cheese, and salami on rye to her, Martha blushed a dusky rose and murmured, "You are the man, and you have not eaten yet."

Longarm snorted, "Aw, mush, set down and dig in like a good Christian, Miss Martha. I told you the two of us were tracking enemies along a dangerous dark trail, and you just now proved you were brave as well as useful."

She plopped down on his side of the hamper to accept her sandwich and exclaim in a pleased voice, "My heart soars to hear you say you have use for me. I have heard so many stories of Wasichu Wastey and his straight tongue and good heart. Is it true you once spoke up for some of our young men who were about to be hanged for stealing some medicine dogs from the blue sleeves?"

To which Longarm could only reply, "Had to. Them cavalry mounts had been run off by Wasichu horse thieves. Wouldn't have been right to hang them Lakota for the deed, ugly as they were."

He rose to fetch those tumblers, and asked her to hold them as he poured. She couldn't protest with her sandwich held between her teeth. So Longarm said, "Yeah, I know it's agin' the rules of your Kit Fox Lodge to thank another for saving your life. But that one cuss didn't have to *cuss me out* for cutting his death song short on him."

She took the grub out of her mouth as he freed one of her hands, and told him, "He was excited. He had never been treated like a man by one of you before, and he didn't know what to say. From a far rise, as they were almost out of sight of that cavalry outpost, he turned to call back in our own tongue that his name was Struck-and-Lived and that he would give you back your own life, if he ever held it in his hand. He said he wasn't sure you heard him."

Longarm washed down some of his creation with hard cider and replied, "I reckon it's the thought that counts. You know this Struck-and-Lived cuss, Miss Martha?"

She nodded soberly and said, "He is my father's sister's son. That is why I was so excited to see you when you first came in downstairs. I can't wait to tell someone who knows someone up at the Rosebud Reservation to tell Struck-and-Lived how I made myself of use to the great Wasichu Wastey!"

Longarm chewed and swallowed some before he sighed and confessed, "I ain't sure how much anything you can tell me about them Cree-speakers staying here will help. Their trail through this hotel seems a mite cold, no offense. But this hamper surely came in useful. So how come you've spread that blanket on the rug?"

She set aside her half-eaten sandwich, placed her drink on the floor near the bed, and rose to her feet, murmuring, "I was afraid you were never going to ask, Wasichu Wastey!"

Then she shucked her one-piece Mother Hubbard off over her head to stride over to the center of the blanket and drop to her naked knees on the shoddy wool, with the nipples of her firm young breasts painted with vermillion as well and all her pubic hairs plucked out, as her older religious notions suggested.

So Longarm set his own grub aside and placed his own hard cider on the floor near hers, figuring they were both going to want something handy to drink mighty soon.

Chapter 11

Longarm forgot all the bad things he'd ever said about the surly Struck-and-Lived as the Lakota's pretty little kinswoman cast her bread upon the waters, as she'd been told to at the mission school. That was what she called it as she pleasured him Lakota style, squatting above him on her heels to milk his old organ-grinder with her tight little ring-dang-doo.

Men who'd learned about birds and bees in tipis didn't ask the gal to get on top because they were lazy. It was much easier on the gal's tailbone than doing it on the ground or a hardwood floor. So she figured Longarm was being considerate by allowing her to do most of the work.

Most, but not all. No man born of mortal woman could have just lain there like a bump on a stump with anything so swell riding to glory with such a sweet grip on the saddlehorn.

It was dark out by then, and they hadn't lit the bed lamp, but enough streetlight came in the open window for him to enjoy the shadowy view as Martha bounced atop him. Human night vision was attuned to motion, and she sure provided some.

They came her way on the blanket. Then Longarm corrupted her morals by doing it some more atop the bed,

Wasichu way. Like a lot of Indian gals, Martha Was-Yellow found kissing a man while he humped her sort of depraved. But she liked it, once she got used to laughing about the way his mustache felt.

She was flattered as hell when he shared a second-wind smoke with her. So seeing he had her in such a friendly, talkative mood, Longarm got them to talking about that card game with a pair of silver-mounted spurs changing hands across the table.

The Lakota gal told him she'd quit for the day before that mystery woman sashayed in with her friend off the college campus. But careful questioning got more out of Martha than one might have expected.

She confirmed that Colorado University was for men only, with its main entrance three blocks further down Broadway, but said she'd heard tell that the northwest reaches of the big triangular campus were a place to meet friends of the opposite sex after classes. She added that she'd had no personal experience with college boys, being what she was, and she'd heard that the campus police chased off obvious hookers.

He asked about less obvious hookers, and she commenced to toy with his virile member as she jokingly replied, "If you showed this to them, hear me, they would not make you pay. I don't know whether the students at UC pay the women they meet after classes on the campus walks. Some of us do cast our bread upon the waters without asking for anything but kind words and good smoking. The clerk donwstairs thought the woman who stayed here with one or more of those Cree-speaking men, as you called them, was a French whore who needed a bath. All of them called her Fifi, and everyone working here suspected all five of them fucked her. A lot."

"Which room were they staying in?" he asked, returning her favor by petting her smooth pubic mound.

She said, "Three rooms on the second floor, 207, 208,

and 209. Two hundred nine was the biggest one, a corner room. I think that is where this card game of yours would have been played. There is one of those tables you call a drop-leaf in that room. It would be big enough for a big game if you pulled it away from the wall and unfolded it. Our night man thought the woman they called Fifi brought other men in with her after dark many times. He thought she was just fucking them for money. She might have been luring them into crooked card games to steal *all* their money!"

Longarm frowned thoughtfully and decided, "It's as good a way to set a mark up with murder evidence, as soon as you study on it. This sure is turning out to be a small world. The Mounties asked for some Denver rider to help 'em track down a suspected Métis gal, and there seems to be a whole nest of the same sprouting just a day's ride outside the Denver city limits!"

He went on to explain the situation up Canada way. She'd heard tell of the Red River Breeds, hadn't considered them Indian, and had always thought they were from south of the Canada line.

She said, "Some used to drive those creaking carts through our old hunting grounds in the Shining Times. I barely remember those Shining Times, but I can still picture those tall-wheeled carts piled high with things we had use for. Our Cheyenne friends could speak to them and act as go-betweens. They treated us better than some Wasichu. They carried looking glasses, brass tacks, red ribbons, and beads of all colors. In the Shining Times we could trade buffalo robes for all sorts of good things and, hear me, they did not try to cheat us. We did not know the redcoats from the north were after them."

Longarm said, "They weren't, if we're talking about no more than a dozen or so years ago when Red Cloud still laid down the law up in the Dakota Territory, which was bigger then. The big fuss up Canada way these days is that, like your nation, the Métis would like to turn the clock back to the way things were before things changed to the way things are today."

The Indian gal sighed and asked, "Why do things have to change? You Wasichu can't seem to leave things the way they have always been. The way things *ought* to be."

Longarm snubbed out the smoke and slid two fingers deeper to gently rock the little fisherman in her canoe as he calmly replied, "Change ain't an invention of my kind alone. Other Indians, ferocious Indians called Apache or Navaho by us, tell of a Holy Being they call Changing Woman. Their way-chanters sing of how Changing Woman only leaves the rocks and bones of the dead unchanged. She causes everything that lives to change and then change some more for the better or the worse. Them way-chanters may be on to something. Over in England there's this Doc Darwin who's been teaching how change might be good for us all in the long run. He holds that the man or beast most fitted to changing times is the one most likely to make it, as his weaker, or dumber, kith and kin go under. I know some Arapaho running a bakery in Denver, and you've got as easy a life here in town as you'd have managed in the Shining Times. So . . ."

"That's not true!" the Indian gal almost wailed, twisting his dong for attention as she protested, "I was little. But I remember. I can still feel the grease running down my chin when we ate and ate and ate after the buffalo runs. I can still remember the young men dancing in the firelight, counting their coups after a good fight. Like those people with creaking carts filled with trade goods, we lived free as the wind and our world was shining, shining, shining!"

Longarm softly said, "Golden memories are pretty lies we tell ourselves, Miss Martha. Childhood memories of white kids—playing marbles and winning, jumping in swimming holes where the water was just right, balmy afternoons just lazing under an apple tree whilst sucking on a grass stem—leave out all the marbles they lost, all the sleepless nights after a serious sunburn, and endless hours of the sheer boredom that goes with a poor boy's upbringing."

He grimaced and said, "Rich kids have their own problems. I've had this same conversation with gals from better backgrounds. Rich kids get toothaches the same as poor kids and Indian kids. The difference is that rich kids get to the dentist sooner. There's something to be said for civilization when you have a toothache, or a busted leg. I remember this Arapaho lady I came across in a rock shelter, not far from here, when I was scouting for the cav during that big Arapaho roundup and removal a few years back. She was in bad shape. Hadn't had a thing to eat for weeks or a drop to drink for days. But we pulled her through easy enough with canteen water, trail rations, and an army surgeon to set her dislocated knee. Her band had left her behind there when she'd hurt herself and just couldn't keep up. There'd been nothing else they could do for her. That was the way things were in their Shining Times. Now they're over in the Indian Territory on the Arapaho Reserve, bitching and moaning of the good old days as they wait for Allotment Day. Doc Darwin would put his money on them Arapaho running that bakery in Denver."

She said she'd rather fornicate some more than argue Indian policy. So that was what they were doing when there came an unexpected knocking at the door.

Longarm rose, grabbing for the six-gun on the bedpost as Martha slithered under the bed, dragging her duds and that blanket after her.

So when a voice from the hall sounded like Crown Sergeant Foster, Longarm opened the door a crack to ask what was up.

Foster took in Longarm's naked appearance at a glance and said, "I see *you're* not! Do you usually turn in this early, Long?"

Longarm let him in, turning away to grab for his seersucker pants over the foot of the bed as he calmly replied, "Not usually. Let me put it another way, you sarcastic cuss. What the fuck's going on!"

Foster said, "You'll never believe who I just spotted down on the college campus!"

Longarm hauled on the pants without underwear, to save time and seeing it was still warm out, as he growled, "Not if you don't tell me, you shy little thing."

Foster said, "You were right about somebody not wanting us here in Boulder. Pete LeClerc was roaming in the gloaming with the other college boys and I know for a fact he's not enrolled at Colorado U! That was one of the things I was asking about when I wired Fort MacLeod a few minutes earlier."

Longarm hadn't taken off his socks to entertain the visitor hiding under his bed. As he hauled on his boots he asked with a puzzled frown, "Constable Pierre Le-Clerc from the border town of Canmont? The lawman who let Bat Masterson take Sister Simone away from him without any fight?"

The burly Mountie nodded grimly and said, "The same. I'd wanted to question him further. But after our one and only interview, LeClerc was simply no longer there. He'd already been sacked by the town council for cowardice. But he was a part-timer with a nearby stud spread, and I was rather surprised to learn he'd sold out, at a loss, and faded away without telling anyone where he might be going."

Longarm rose to put a shirt on and button up as he nodded and said, "Well, you all called me in on the case because Sister Simone had been headed south in line with the Rockies, and I've met up with heaps of your rebel Métis all along that route as far south as the Panhandle. So we're talking about a payoff, right?"

The Mountie said, "That's what it looks like. LeClerc had to lock her up when his honest deputy, poor Grouleau, brought her in on suspicion. He had to turn in the money and stolen goods in her cart, and impound the cart, because Grouleau and that other deputy, O'Day, had tallied it all up and set it all down on paper. So the pay-off, or the promise of a payoff, came later, possibly from Sister Simone in the flesh. Nobody else saw that mysterious gunman claiming to be Bat Masterson leaving with her. LeClerc sent his two deputies out of town after dark and simply let her go. How do you like that so far?"

Longarm reached for his gun rig and strapped it on, saying, "Works for me. Get to your bumping into LeClerc this evening."

Foster said, "I didn't. I'd asked around, and they told me at a saloon across from UC Main that such action as there was on the campus grounds seemed most likely in the northwest corner of the same. So I drifted over that way in this rather juvenile summer outfit. LeClerc was seated on a bench under a lamppost. He barely glanced up as I passed. He didn't recognize me in this unusual uniform. I drifted on, circled to his rear, and sat on another bench shaded by a clump of cottonwood."

Longarm put on his hat and asked, "So then?"

"A woman came by to pause as if asking directions. LeClerc rose to show her the way, or pick her up, as I assume the charade was meant to be recalled by any possible witnesses."

Longarm said, "Let's go. You did trail them somewhere sensible before you dropped off their trail to come back here, I hope?"

Foster said, "This is the hotel I trailed them to. They're one flight below, in Room 303. From the gay sounds of laughter through the door, I'd say they mean to be there for a time."

Longarm blinked and demanded, "Not LeClerc and the one and original Sister Simone?"

The Mountie snorted, "I'd have arrested her on sight, of course. I don't have a charge against LeClerc just yet.

I've no idea who the doxie he picked up on the college campus could be."

Longarm dropped to his hands and knees to ask Martha, under the bed. The Lakota gal, who worked there, whispered, "Her name is DuPrix. She arrived alone this afternoon, ahead of you two."

Longarm strightened back up to tell the Mountie, "French-sounding name, traveling lonesome. Do you have anybody named DuPrix on your wanted list?"

Crown Sergeant Foster replied with a puzzled frown, "Not that I recall. Who were you asking just now?"

Longarm said, "There's this troll as lives under my bed. What say we get on down to 303 and . . . then what, bust in right off or listen a spell?"

His question was answered not by Foster, but by the dulcet roar of gunfire. A .32 repeating whore pistol from the sounds of the shots.

As the two lawmen ran for the stairwell, they heard high heels already running downstairs. Longarm snapped, "I'll take 303. You go after *her*, seeing you know what she looks like!"

Foster didn't argue. On the next landing down, they split up that way, with Foster never pausing as he ran downstairs and Longarm on his way as fast along the hall runner to an open doorway with smoke still curling around the jam.

Another hall door opened and Longarm snapped, "Get back and stay back in the name of the law!" So the curious guest crawfished back inside as Longarm tore into 303, six-gun in hand.

He paused in the middle of the lamplit room to mutter, "Aw, shit!" as he stared down at the naked cuss half in and half out of bed with a chagrined expression on his face and a row of four bullet holes up his bare belly, oozing hardly any blood.

Bullet holes were like that when the muzzle blast had cauterized and blackened bare flesh at close range.

Chapter 12

Longarm was opening closets and drawers and finding them empty when Foster rejoined him with the night clerk and the Boulder copper badge who'd responded to the gunshots.

As he looked at the body sprawled half on and half off the bedstead, the Mountie said, "She got away down the alley out back. So now we know Constable LeClerc let Sister Simone go and this is how they paid him off, the poor simp!"

Longarm said, "He had a trusting nature for even a part-time lawman, but I doubt this was planned for here and now."

Turning to the local lawman, he asked, "Is it safe to guess the town of Boulder has this hotel down as a second-rate transient hotel where nothing amazing usually takes place?"

The clerk, a young jasper likely working his way through college with a night job, sputtered, "We've never had a killing or a serious brawl since I've been working here!"

The copper badge smiled thinly and backed the kid, sort of, when he said, "Mostly whiskey drummers and paid-off trail hands passing through. We got wilder hotels by far downwind of the stockyards to the east of the campus. That's where the boys go to get really dirty."

Foster asked what a local lawman knew about other back doors along that dark alley out back.

The Boulder roundsman said, "I can see how you'd lose anyone in a hurry who knew this part of town. There's the back doors of three other hotels and four rooming houses. In desperation she might have ducked into a shit house behind either the Bear Mountain or El Dorado Saloon. Her best bet would have been the vacant lot breaking the back row of buildings to the north. If she had the balls and you were really hot on her heels, she could have risked flattening out in the waist-high weeds and—"

"I never checked that route," the Mountie cut in, disgusted with himself as he dropped to one knee. "I went for those street lamps at the far end of the alley the way a bluegill strikes at a baited safety pin."

As he bent low to peer under the bed, a comical sight in seersucker pants, the copper badge asked what he was looking for.

Foster muttered, "Trolls," before he hauled out a lady's carpetbag and rose to carry it to a writing table across from the corpse. Longarm asked the night clerk if that bag went with the missing Miss DuPrix.

Longarm had known how to pronounce that, having met up with French talkers in his time. But even though he'd just said, "Doo Pree," the room clerk said, "I wasn't on duty when Madame Duh Pricks arrived. I don't know who else it could belong to, though."

Foster dumped the contents out on the green blotter. There were four frilly snot rags, an eyebrow pencil, half a box of .32 rounds, a douche bag, and some black lace unmentionables. Only one of her shimmy shirts had a label. It said she'd bought the lacy garment in Montreal.

Longarm told the Boulder lawman Foster was a Canadian lawman, working on a puzzle involving border-jumping Red River Breeds.

The Colorado lawman said, "I read about them putting down some sort of revolution up yonder. What are them fugitive rebels doing this far south? Wasn't there something in the papers about the Canadian law finding a whole bunch of rebel leaders settled in Montana Territory? And didn't our own State Department tell Queen Victoria to go fuck herself?"

As the Canadian Mountie shot him a ferocious look, Longarm quickly explained, "They told Her Majesty's Dominion Government to do that. Their own Boss Macdonald said some awfully mean things about us before we took to telling *him* to go fuck himself. You catch more flies with honey than with vinegar, and so far Louis Riel, the rebel leader now teaching school up Montana way, ain't been dumb enough to piss President Hayes and his Lemonade Lucy off."

"Then what are Canadian rebels doing this far south, shooting folks on my beat?" the Boulder law in all its majesty demanded.

It was a good question. Longarm said, "I might have just answered that. Partway, at least. Their known leaders are under the constant if casual eye of Uncle Sam's other deputies up Montana way. Somebody, with or without orders from Riel or the other leaders, has other fish to fry well south of the border. Before you ask, we don't have the least notion who might be up to what. Have you ever had the feeling you were missing pieces of the puzzle, or looking at the ones you had all wrong?"

Foster turned from the evidence piled on the writing table to stare thoughtfully at the corpse across the room as he mused, half to himself, "She took her gun with her. It sounded like the sort of small-caliber pistol ladies of the evening carry for emergencies, and so what was the emergency here?"

Longarm pointed his jaw at the naked LeClerc to suggest, "Him. If she'd lit out naked, an amusing picture, her duds would still be here and she wouldn't have been able to run so freely into the night. What say our Madame DuPrix was sent as a courier to pick this corrupt shit up where they'd told him to just sit and wait."

"Why was he a corrupt shit?" asked the local lawman.

Foster said, "Later. I like what you're suggesting, Long. Sister Simone or her fictitious Bat Masterson told LeClerc to just make his way here to a college town, have a seat on the campus, and wait there until someone came for him. If I do say so myself, I was watching the bench rather cleverly from some distance when she thought it safe to make contact. Then she brought him here to this hotel they'd used on earlier occasions to . . . Your turn."

Longarm said, "*Relay* him some more. Whether they were planning on killing him or recruiting a known bad apple, they weren't going to do so here at this hotel. They never harmed a hair of Jack Carter's head here at this hotel. They suckered him up to Collins and handed him to the law on a silver platter, or bearing silver spurs leastways."

The Boulder lawman said he'd heard about them catching the killer of Gustav Persson. Foster told him to shut up and turned back to Longarm to agree. "They've been trying to divert attention to the north of here by jiggling their hook in Fort Collins. But what will you bet they're sitting on the bank here in Boulder!"

"Maybe Denver, one rail stop away with even more doorways to duck through," said Longarm. Nodding at the naked corpse of LeClerc, he took a deep breath and said, "See how you like this. Leave whatever Sister Simone and her gang are up to on the back of the stove for now. Say Sister Simone was caught trying to sneak across the border with cash and stolen property in her Red River cart. Say two honest young lawmen hauled her and her property before an underpaid part-time constable who wasn't as honest. He'd have to turn in the money she had on her because it had already been recorded by the arresting officers. So she must have promised him something else. Given her bad habits with wine bottles, she likely offered hot jars of honey and plenty of money for the loss of a job that didn't pay much to begin with. So LeClerc sent his two deputies out of town after dark, and simply turned Sister Simone loose after one of the fellow travelers who'd been riding one of them ponies tethered to her cart showed up, claiming to be the rough and tough Bat Masterson."

Longarm started to reach for a smoke, considered how many he'd have to offer all around, and dropped his hand to continue. "Using the name of a known Canadian gunslick might have been a slip. Hardly anyone outside of Colorado knew the real Masterson is in Trinidad these days. I'd say that lets Louis Riel and the original leaders of the Metís cause off the hook."

"Why do you say that?" asked the Canadian lawman.

Longarm modestly replied, "Same reasons your superiors at Fort MacLeod requested my help as a lawman who might be able to get into a friendlier conversation than you with Canadian rebels. I told you I've met up with Riel and some of his inner circle. I could tell you a tale of some pleasant times in a Red River cart, but that's agin' a gentleman's code. My point is that they know me as well, and they know I ride herd on this neck of the woods. So why would they set up some sort of secret operation close to Denver instead of dozens of towns as big and closer to Canada where I'd be less likely to trip over a familiar face or figure?"

"Do you know Sister Simone, or this mysterious Madame DuPrix, on sight?" asked the Mountie dryly.

Longarm said, "I said I knew a heap of Métis rebels. Not *all* of 'em. As to Madame DuPrix, I don't know whether I've ever seen her before or not. What did she look like this evening?"

Foster said, "French, small, cameo features at the distance I was from them by lamplight."

The night clerk volunteered, "A real looker, and sort of ladylike in her manner. Made you feel she was doing you a great honor when you fetched her more soap."

Foster made a wry face and pointed out, "They were snickering dirty when we listened at yonder door earlier."

Longarm said, "There you go. She was trying to laugh it off as they wrestled less rough, at first. We've all of us wrestled with a gal who kept making up excuses about her folks coming in, a little sister that might be watching, and so on, until we saw she didn't want to and gave up. So what if this hot-natured shit, after working his way down here slow and sneaky, had his heart set on more of the free samples Sister Simone had handed out in Canmont? What if this Madame DuPrix really *is* a lady, or wants to be, and what if he just wouldn't take no for an answer whilst they were waiting here for other members of the gang to show up and take him off her hands and out of her hair?"

Foster said, "That works! Say he stripped himself bare to come at her in earnest as she pleaded in vain she was not that sort of girl! Say he'd already decided she *was* the kind of girl who'd pose with a bottle up her twat and a nun's wimple on her head. One can see how he'd take her for a prick-teasing harlot, while she was taking him for a sex maniac. So . . . I say, if she shot him without orders in a hitherto safe hideout . . ."

"She could be in deep shit!" Longarm agreed with a nod. "She might *know* she's in deep shit. We might be able to get her to talk if we can catch up with her before *they* do!"

Foster asked the night clerk if they'd sent for the meat wagon. The kid said that was the roundsman's job. The copper badge said it was no such thing. The coroner, like the sheriff, was an elected official of the county, not the township.

Longarm told the Mountie to let Boulder County and Boulder Township sort it out, seeing they had a train to catch.

As they were headed down the stairwell the British subject made a snide comment on Yankee jurisprudence. Having rowed for Harrow, Foster was good at being snide.

Longarm said, "It's a bother, I know. Is it true what I hear about Her Majesty having to ask permission from the Lord Mayor every time she wants to drive into the heart of London Town?"

"God will get you for that!" Her Majesty's lawman said with a laugh in spite of himself.

Out front, a horse-drawn ambulance had drawn up and, as they broke out a litter, one of the crew asked what Longarm and Foster could tell him about a shooting at that address.

Longarm replied, "Neither one of us was mixed up in it. I hear it was on the third floor." Since this was the simple truth when you studied on it, the two lawmen legged it back across the creek for the Walnut Street Station. They could hear the tolling of an engine bell long before they could get there, and once they got there, it was too late. The ticket agent at one end of the dinky waiting room told them the Denver-bound local crowded with college boys out for some bright lights and dark doings had just left.

Foster swore and decided, "We could wire your friends on the Denver Force and they could get to the Denver depot in plenty of time, eh, what?"

Longarm said, "Worth a try. How do you want me to describe a particular young gal getting off a train mixed in with a college outing?"

Foster said he'd send the wire, and turned from the ticket window to get cracking. There was something to be said for standing with your back to the doorway of a public waiting room in seersucker when those with just cause to worry about you have you pictured in a red tunic and black riding breeches. For neither of the sort of breathless riders dashing into the waiting room recognized Crown Sergeant Foster first.

It was still a near thing as Foster snapped, "Surrender in the Queen's High Name!" and went for his .455.

He nailed the second one. He'd have never beaten the first one to the draw. But thanks to Longarm having noticed Foster tensing to draw before he declared such intentions loud and clear, the sidewinder-quick one wearing a Pendelton shirt and a low-slung S&W Schofield .45 shot into the floor, instead of into Foster, as Longarm cleaned his plow with a lucky shot that went in one ear and out the other.

As the two lawmen stood alone above the two sprawled forms on the floorboards of the smoke-filled waiting room, Longarm laconically observed, "I never yell a warning when there's more than one of 'em. Why did we just now shoot these total strangers, pard?"

Foster as calmly replied, "They weren't strangers to *me*. Allow me to present Trapper Jack MacBean and Black Pierre Moreau, both wanted for crimes against the laws of man and nature. They were reputed to be bisexual, but then most men who spend most of their adult lives in prison tend to be. You'll have to forgive them for not offering to shake. As you can see, they're somewhat indisposed at the moment."

Longarm smiled crookedly and decided, "You're really enjoying your snide-ass self over this shoot-out, ain't you?"

To which Crown Sergeant Foster replied without a hint of shame, "Yes, I really am. We promised a raped child's mother that the Mounties always get their man. I can't wait to wire Fort MacLeod that I just got *two* of them, all the way out of our country!"

Longarm said, "I'll watch the store here whilst you send all them wires. If I were you I'd wire Denver Police about that Madame DuPrix before I bragged about these two. She's still on the run. These gunslicks ain't going nowheres now without our permission. But what will you bet they were after that French gal, and who do you reckon Sister Simone's gang is likely to send after her as soon as they find out these two let her get away alive?"

Chapter 13

It was a good thing they were so close to the Denver District Court, where most everybody who could read took the *Denver Post* or *The Rocky Mountain News,* for even as he was telling the tale to the brace of Boulder County deputies in a waiting room that still reeked of gun smoke, Longarm was aware he was commencing to sound like that comical stage routine where the town constable is questioning the hobo, who answers "Where have you come from?" with "I ain't too sure," and then "Where are you headed?" with "I don't know."

Longarm had had the sense to pin his federal badge on and put his reloaded six-gun away before he had to explain those dead men on the station floor, and the ticket clerk backed him up when he told them the rascals had spurned an attempt to arrest them peaceably.

They still thought Foster should have stayed around, seeing he'd shot at least one of the poor bastards. But before the argument could get heated, Foster came back, saying, "I say, if you ever want to feel like a horse's neck, try wiring some Yank lawmen you don't know to be on the lookout for a suspect you can only describe as a fairly nice-looking brunette at some distance in uncertain light!"

Longarm introduced him as Crown Sergeant Foster of the RCMP to the Boulder deputies. Foster told them he'd wired Canada about the shootout, and told Longarm he'd asked Fort MacLeod to send them a copy of that dirty picture of Sister Simone and her sisters in sin.

One of the Boulder deputies protested that they hadn't shot the men on the floor in Canada. Longarm said, "Don't push to where someone has call to push back. The two of us outrank the two of you in the eyes of Queen Victoria *and* Uncle Sam."

The one deputy who seemed to be having trouble with his manners that evening said, "Your fucking rank don't mean shit in the eyes of Boulder County! You two outsiders just now shot two local residents and—"

"Bullshit! They were fugitives from Canadian justice!" roared the irate Crown Sergeant Foster.

Longarm suggested to the deputy, "I told you not to push it, pard. If this blows up in your face, I'll just have to testify at the inquest that you were warned you were rawhiding a man who'd just survived a gunfight with a known killer and wasn't ready to play schoolyard games with a self-important jackass!"

"Who do you think you're calling a jackass!" gasped the blustering county lawman.

To which Longarm wearily replied, "If you don't want to be called a jackass don't act like one. The two of us know the rules better than you do. They call for us to turn in signed depositions and if called upon, appear before your county coroner's inquest when he, not you, has the authority to convene one."

The Boulder deputy looked down at the dead bodies, blushing like a gal who'd just farted on a porch swing, and spoke softer as he said, "Look, we have to turn in our own reports and what you've told us, so far, don't make a whole lot of sense!"

Longarm said, "If it made sense to us we'd have made some arrests by this time!"

So they all simmered down, got the two gunslicks to the morgue to spend the night there with the late Constable LeClerc, and Longarm and Foster went back to the Flatiron Hotel.

Longarm failed to find little Martha Was-Yellow in or under his bed. So he jawed some more with the night clerk, caught some sleep, and got an early start after breakfast. Foster headed back to the Western Union. Longarm headed for the county clerk's office. Neither one was looking forward to the coroner's inquest, set for the afternoon, but it only took a few minutes to dig up and write down some matters of public record. Once he'd done this, Longarm got his cleaned and pressed tobacco-tweed outfit from that tailor, pinned his badge to the lapel, and legged it east to the fashionable rise called Mapleton Hill, where the houses had mansard roofs, corner turrets, and liveried household help.

The snooty butler who came to the front door of the mustard-colored Elliot house would have looked down on Longarm if he'd been half tall enough. But all he could manage was to usher the lawman into a drawing room and tell him to wait there.

So Longarm waited, admiring some fantailed goldfish on a stand in the bay window, and then a brown-haired gal with a pretty face and a need to lose a few pounds came in, wearing black poplin, to declare she was the niece and the executor of the late Red Jim Elliot—who'd died of pneumonia in February owning half of Boulder, according to a less-well-rounded young gal at the county clerk's.

The pleasantly plump one in black said to call her Flora Bell, her late uncle being on her own mother's side, and invited Longarm to sit down beside her on a settee overlooking the goldfish. He asked in a desperately casual tone if he was correct in guessing both last names might be of the Scottish persuasion.

She said they sure were, and would have rung for some

tea if Longarm hadn't stopped her, saying he was in a rush. He told her about the doings at the Flatiron Hotel, leaving Martha Was-Yellow out, of course, and got right down to brass tacks, saying, "It's my understanding that your late uncle, or his estate, owns not only that Flatiron Hotel but the Bear Mountain Saloon, two back doors down the alley from the same."

Flora Bell answered easily, "We may own the property, if you say so. My poor Uncle Jim was a real-estate developer, not an innkeeper or bartender. He and my late Aunt Maggie got in on the ground floor when Boulder was no more than the crossroads of Broadway and Pearl, with the Walnut Street Station still a dream. They bought vacant lots cheap, put buildings on them, and rented them out dear. We don't manage any of the lives or businesses of our tenants. I believe that hotel over by the college is staffed and operated by some French people. There are lots of French people in the hotel and restaurant businesses. You'd have to ask my rental agent, Mr. Frazer. Tom Frazer."

Longarm nodded and said, "I mean to, ma'am. What about that saloon just down the alley?"

She allowed she'd never been to either address, and asked what the Bear Mountain Saloon might have to do with that killing in the Flatiron Hotel.

Longarm explained, "The killer gal ran out the back because the night clerk never saw her run out the front. She had a well-legged-up lawman hot on her heels. She'd have never made it to the end of that alley before he tore out the same back door of the hotel. So she must have gone somewhere else. At the county clerk's I just now found out that the saloon occupies the first floor and basement of that Elliot estate-owned property. There's a second story, built to serve as the living quarters of the saloon keeper, I suspicion."

She just looked blank.

He said, "Your city directory lists the current addresses

110

of all law-abiding residents, and there's nobody living above the Bear Mountain Saloon officially at present. The saloon below is run by a family of the Irish persuasion who all live together in a bigger hired house up the other side of the creek."

She still didn't seem to follow his drift. He patiently explained, "There's almost always a separate outside entrance to an upstairs flat of rooms. A gal going lickety-split in French heels might have had just enough time to get on up yonder by the time Sergeant Foster got out to that dark alley. I doubt she left a light in the window to show him the way. I could get a search warrant by noon if I had to. But I thought it might be quicker, and easier, to just ask."

She rose to her feet, saying, "Let's do that then. I confess you have me in a state of unrest about all these dire doings on Elliot property! We'll take my carriage to our rental office at Broadway and Pearl and I'll introduce you to Tom Frazer myself!"

So they stepped out in the hall, she called for her carriage in a pleasant but no-nonsense tone, and they waited on the front veranda until a coach and four with a Mexican or Indian driver came around from the back to take them downtown.

It wasn't that far. But ladies of her station weren't expected to walk more than a city block. That was doubtless why so many ladies of her station needed whalebone corsets and considerable help getting into the latest fashions.

The rental office of Elliot Enterprises was on the second story above a bank that rented from them as well. As she swept in with Longarm following, Flora Bell told the clerk gal sweetly but firmly that they'd come to ask her boss, Mr. Frazer, to show them around one of her properties down by the UC campus.

When the washed-out blandly pretty clerk said her boss was out of the office on business, the lady he worked for said she wanted the keys to that rental the Bear Mountain Saloon occupied.

Nobody argued. A few minutes later, at Longarm's direction, they'd driven up the alley behind the Flatiron Hotel, where sure enough, an outside staircase led to a back door above the saloon.

Longarm asked for the keys, and told the swarthy driver to move on along the alley a ways with his boss lady, explaining, "I want you both out of the line of fire if this visit receives a warmer welcome than I'm hoping for."

Then he dropped out to head up the stairs with the keys in his left hand and his .44–40 in the right.

He knocked, standing to one side of the jamb as he knocked some more and told them to open in the name of the law.

When a brogue from below asked what he was talking about, Longarm called down, "Not you. The folks staying up here above your saloon."

The brogue called back, "Sure and there's nobody up there at all at all."

Longarm unlocked the second-story door and followed his gun muzzle through it fast, to crab sideways out of the light with his back to the wallpaper as he threw down on . . . nothing much.

There was a double layer of mock Oriental rugs, as if someone felt no call to disturb the regulars in the saloon below. You could see where once upon a time pictures had hung on the spinach-green and dusky-rose floral wallpaper. But save for a beat-up sofa and four bentwood chairs around a card table, that room was unfurnished.

It seemed as if they'd never had a kitchen. As he followed his gun muzzle forward he found that the other rooms, four more to begin with in a row off a side hall, had been cut by partitions into smaller four-foot-wide chambers.

"Crib house, cheap and dirty," Longarm muttered

aloud as he made sure there was no other way out.

"What's a crib house?" asked Flora Bell from a doorway with a dumb smile on her pleasant moon face.

Longarm said, "I asked you to stay in your carriage with good cause, Miss Flora. It appears the Duffys downstairs are running a respectable saloon at this address these days. One of your uncle's earlier tenants had some shadier business going on in his converted living quarters."

"You mean they were running a *whorehouse* on our property?" she exclaimed before Longarm was braced for it.

He gulped and replied, "That's what some might call it. It's more customary to say parlor house, house of ill repute, or even house of shame. But since you've called a spade a spade, I think somebody recalled the bad old days when Boulder was a-building and construction crews had more pocket jingle than manners. Knowing these premises were no longer occupied as a residence or . . . place of business, they've been using it as an overnight hideout along a getaway trail. Owlhoot riders who've been given the directions are met by a guide pretending to be a casual flirtation over on the campus grounds. From there they're taken to the hotel up the alley to wait some more whilst gang members scout their backtrail and decide what's to be done with them. After they've been approved to move on down the owlhoot trail, they're taken here to this tighter hideout, to wait for whatever further moves the gang has in mind."

"What gang are you talking about?" she almost wailed. "I don't see how anyone could hope to get away with anything as sassy as you say! This second story might be empty, but it's still a rental property. On the market as such! What would have happened if our Tom Frazer had shown up with those keys and a prospective tenant while all this rooting-tooting owlhoot shooting was going on?"

Longarm said, "They'd have been in an awkward fix. So they must not have expected anyone working for you to pester them. That mysterious Madame DuPrix must have known this place was empty last night. She'd have never run to meet up with the other members of her gang after what happened at the hotel. She may have had some of her own belongings up here. We know she was anxious to avoid *us* as well as her fellow gang members. So she hid here long enough to throw old Sergeant Foster off her trail. Then she ran on before any of her firmer pals could . . . Hold it, they'd never come here, once they heard of the killing up the alley. They'll never come here again. Now that we know they used to, blast their sneaky souls!"

Flora Bell hadn't been paying full attention. She demanded, "What was that about Tom Frazer never showing up as they were using Elliot real estate as an outlaw whorehouse?"

He smiled thinly and said, "Hideout. The word you're searching for is hideout, albeit some slap-and-tickle might have been enjoyed by all if half the things they say about Sister Simone is true. As to your Tom Frazer, if that's his name, I'd sure like to talk to him about the way he's been riding herd on your uncle's property since it got to be just an *estate*. Am I correct in assuming that when your uncle died, his rental agent offered the comforting words that he'd manage things the way he always had, the way your uncle would have wanted?"

She said, "Oh, Dear Lord, those were almost his exact words!"

Longarm holstered his six-gun and gently took her by one elbow to herd her back toward the outside stairs as he told her, "I want you to give me his home address. Then I want you to drive home and stay there till you hear from me, or my estate."

She said, "But Deputy Long . . ."

So he cut in. "My friends call me Custis and I don't

want you to but me no buts, Miss Flora. I hope your Tom Frazer has an explanation that holds water. I don't see how he could, and the folks your rental agent seems to have been aiding and abetting are beyond simply mean into mad-dog dangerous!"

Chapter 14

Tom Frazer wasn't at the rooming house owned by the Elliot estate. The bay thoroughbred hunter he'd kept at a nearby livery seemed to be missing, along with the pigskin flat-saddle he'd kept handy in their tack room. One of the stable hands recalled that the rental agent had been by before dawn, saying he had to ride down to Saddle Rock on business. Longarm doubted that was where he'd headed.

Crown Sergeant Foster caught up with Longarm at the county courthouse, where he was going over business ledgers in their reading room. Foster sat down across from him to say, "The Denver police weren't able to stop Madame DuPrix, if that was her name. Trapper Jack and Black Pierre were both born in Canada, but neither was Métis. Moreau was just plain French Canadian, or Quebecois. Trapper Jack MacBean didn't even have that excuse. What if it was just one of those things? The two of them *were* wanted in Canada and I *am* a Canadian Mounted Police officer. So—"

"Too tight a coincidence," Longarm cut in. "I've been thrown off by a chance meeting with a want I wasn't trailing in my time. But we were hot on that DuPrix gal's murderous heels, and the two of them were *chasing* somebody when they came tearing into the waiting room a few minutes after her train pulled out of the station. It's safe to suppose all three of them were likely of the Canadian persuasion. So a gang of impure Canadians instead of dedicated rebel halfbreeds makes more sense than a one-in-a-million chance meeting with a Mountie this far south of the Canadian border! What kind of a name is Frazer? Does it always have to be Scottish?"

The Mountie started to nod, but shook his head. "Depends on how you spell it. The famous Highland clan claims descent from a Norman nobleman granted land by the Ardri Dai, or High King David. But should you spell it Friseur, as it may have been spelled by Norman nobles, it's naturally French. Why do you ask?"

Longarm brought him up to date. Foster stared goggled-eyed and demanded, "What are we doing in this musty reading room? Why didn't you scout me up at once so we could ride after the bounder?"

"Where?" asked Longarm simply. He pointed to his open notebook on the table between them as he continued. "They had all night to plan a mass escape. Given a good lead on a fast horse along well-traveled trails in fair-settled country, that two-faced rental agent could be most anywhere by this time, and we don't even know who else was in on whatever with him. That's what I'm trying to figure with all these tedious county records. Hunting on horseback is fun, hunting on foot is all right, and hunting on paper is a pain in the ass. But sometimes it's the only trail an outlaw's left you."

The more formally educated Mountie nodded soberly and said, "I know the feeling. Why does old paper smell dustier than the prairie in high summer? What have you found out so far?"

"Not a hell of a lot." Longarm sighed. "Our missing rental agent was managing real estate all over Boulder County for the Elliot estate. I doubt we'll find anybody hiding out in any of the vacant quarters I've unearthed so far. He was too slick to leave a whole house or building empty. Kids looking to scare up a ghost, or tramps out to salvage pipes to peddle, are likely to come snooping around a neighborhood haunted house. But nobody notices an unrented second story over a barbershop or saloon open for business, whilst neither your average barber or barkeep gives a damn about who might live upstairs when they don't own the building. I found eight such possible hideouts here in Boulder. Last night, when she filled Constable LeClerc with lead, our Madame DuPrix must have inspired some hasty packing. They'd know that once we turned one rock over at the Flatiron Hotel, we'd just keep turning others over, one at a time. It's no wonder the gal ran for her life. I'm sure Sister Simone will tell her she should have put out, before they shoot her."

Foster nodded. "Then if we can get to this Madame DuPrix before *they* do, she'll surely see it's in her best interest to tell us all we want to know, eh, what?"

Longarm made a wry face and pointed out, "Her lawyer won't let her confess to killing LeClerc unless we can offer her a defense-of-honor deal. But since that's likely what happened . . . I wonder what that poor sick puppy wanted her to *do!*"

"Isn't that obvious?" asked the Canadian with a lofty expression.

Longarm said, "Not hardly. The gal's been running with outlaws led or mayhaps just pleasured by Sister Simone, if not other sisters in sin. So on the face of it, Constable LeClerc was done in by a whore he asked too much of. I reckon everybody has some line they just won't cross. Few if any parlor houses will let a Chinaman through the door, and some gals refuse to kiss a customer no matter what else they may do for him. That night up to Canmont when LeClerc and Sister Simone made friends whilst his deputies were away must have been one wild night to remember. But we'll have to catch Sister Simone, or at least Madame DuPrix, if we're ever going to know for certain. As of now, the poor shit's dead, his killer and all her associates here in Boulder seem to have scattered, and we still have that dumb inquest to attend this afternoon!"

So they did, and the county coroner admitted he couldn't make heads nor tails of it, even with the new information about Tom Frazer thrown in.

When he considered calling Flora Bell in to speak for the Elliot estate, Longarm talked him out of it. That would have called for yet another tedious hearing, and as he told the coroner and his panel, the propery owned by the late Red Jim Elliot at the time of his death, and managed since by his niece, executrix, and heiress through a rental agent she'd never hired, was literally an open book. Everything the estate possessed was on the county tax rolls. No property had changed hands since her uncle had passed away naturally. Longarm couldn't see how the gal would offer any testimony different from what had been provided by her two-faced rental agent.

Flora Bell must have had friends in the courthouse gang. The hearing was over by four-thirty. There was an invitation to supper in Longarm's pigeonhole when he got back to his hotel. It said he could bring Sergeant Foster if he wanted to. But Foster was off to canvas all the liveries in town, as if he expected an owlhoot rider to leave a forwarding address, even when he or she rode off suddenly and suspiciously.

Foster couldn't seem to get it through his head that the state of Colorado, this close to its capital city of Denver, offered many more places to ride for than the Canadian West up around Fort MacLeod. Nobody with a lick of sense was going to ride the high country and risk leaving a trail when they could hole up indoors or catch a train out to most anywhere.

As he got cleaned up to call on a lady, Longarm reflected on that angle as the motive for all these secret meetings in a college town just outside of Denver. They hadn't *wanted* him and Foster to look for Sister Simone this far south. They'd tried to convince everyone the action was closer to the border, up by Collins, where they'd . . . killed that rich Swede and stolen his spurs?

As he shaved, he told his face in the pier glass, "Try her this way. The gang had nothing directly to do with that robbery. Being in the trade of dishonest dealings, one of Sister Simone's pals came by them spurs dishonestly, playing cards or just stealing from some other owlhoot rider. He may have bitched right out that he couldn't sell or hock such fine spurs because of them initials and the fame of a former owner."

As Longarm washed his face clean he decided, "However they come by them, they used them as a red herring to draw suspicion north, closer to the scene of that crime. Then they gunned an innocent pawnbroker in mock revenge to make it seem more certain they were headquartered up around Fort Collins instead of here in Boulder!"

"To do what?" was the question he just had no answer for as he headed over to Mapleton Hill to sing for his supper.

The pleasingly plump Flora Bell served up a fine feed, or had it served for them as they sat at opposite ends of a table covered with white linen and enough silver service to tempt border raiders. They dined on mock turtle soup and real Pacific oysters, shipped on ice from Frisco Bay, not mountain oysters, cut from spring lambs. After that, they ate pork chops served with asparagus and apple sauce with mashed potatoes. She asked if he'd had enough "on tray," and suggested they take their just desserts in the parlor. When he said he was game, she shyly allowed she was trying to cut back on full-course suppers for her health. He didn't say whether he thought she was getting fat or not. It was none of his business.

Out in the parlor, a different one, with ferns instead of goldfish in the bay window, the same stout maid served them coffee and those fancy French cakes they called petits fours. When he told her he'd had some of that swell Scotch shortbread at the Tabor Mansion in Denver, when he'd foiled a burglary there with Sergeant Nolan of the Denver police, she looked pained and said, "I heard our Silver Dollar Horace Tabor favors bagpipe bands and keeps a wee beastie his wife doesn't know about on the side. We're living in America now."

Which made Longarm wonder why they were having petits fours for dessert.

Nibbling and sipping as the darkness gathered inside and out, with nobody coming in to light the parlor lamps, Longarm brought the lady of the house up to date on the hearing he'd just attended. She said he'd been a dear to keep her name out of it, and asked, "What do you think Tom Frazer was really up to? Since his office assistant, Nora, came crying to me this afternoon about your last visit, the two of us have gone over the books, and frankly, we couldn't find anything wrong with them!"

Longarm nodded and said, "Neither could I when I spent some time at the county clerk's. It appears Frazer deposited all the rent money he collected to your uncle's estate account. You'd allowed him to go on as before, drawing expenses as well as salaries for himself and his office help from a separate expense account. He could have cooked the books a mite, but any serious stealing would have been easy to spot, given a finite list of tenants with rents owed and collected in plain red and black ink. Your uncle's estate lost a little on those properties he could have rented but didn't. The losses don't add up to serious embezzlement. Frazer seems to have done no more than let some pals hide out in officially vacant quarters. It only commences to sound serious as soon as you consider the sort of pals he was hiding out. Madame DuPrix was a killer for certain. Trapper Jack and Black Pierre were killers for hire. Sister Simone seems to be dedicated to pure evil. According to the Mounties, she's been mixed up in everything from the sale of French postcards to inciting to riot and armed robbery!"

She wanted to hear more about the wicked renegade nun. Most folks who heard of Sister Simone did.

So he told her as much as he knew, leaving out some details such as self-abuse with wine bottles. When the gal who owned the property the Flatiron Hotel stood on asked if he thought Sister Simone had stayed there, Longarm said, "The late Jack Carter, or Jacques Cartier, said so. He testified she lured him there, got him into a poker game so's he could win those fatal spurs, and then kept him there, drunk and happy, until they could frame him for murder in Fort Collins."

Flora looked so unsettled in the gathering dusk that Longarm told her, "She ain't on your property now. She was overheard in Fort Collins saying she was on her way back to her nunnery. We figure she hides out with an unsuspecting RC teaching order betwixt flings. Would you like me to light a lamp in here, Miss Flora?"

She said, "No, it's not that dark yet. How would it be possible for any girl to lead a double life as a wanton outlaw and any sort of nun?"

He said, "She'd have to be two-faced as all get-out. She might not really lead any outlaw gang. From the little we know for certain, she could be the mighty dirty doxie, even a part-time dirty doxie, of some really bad apple.

"There's some dispute as to who was really in charge of the Tunstall-McSween guns during that recent Lincoln County War, with more than one old-timer doubting young Henry McCarty, the so-called Billy the Kid, was more than a young hand with an interesting handle for the reporters to play with. Dick Brewer, the foreman of the Tunstall spread, makes more sense as the leader them other young hands were following during their early wins. The tide turns with Buckshot Roberts and Dick Brewer killing one another in the same gunfight, leaving nobody more responsible than young Billy to carry on.

"Some say it was Cole Younger, not Frank nor Jesse, who planned all them robberies up until they picked the wrong bank in Northfield. Ain't it odd how neither Frank nor Jesse have done all that much since old Cole and his brothers got captured and claimed that they'd only followed orders from a ferocious kid called Jesse?"

"Then who do you think the real mastermind might be? Tom Frazer?" she asked in a worried tone.

He said, "Not hardly. He's been at his desk here in Boulder a lot of times when Sister Simone's busted out of her nunnery. It's just possible Tom Frazer has some Canadian connections. It's downright likely he's been working hand in glove with the gang she leads or runs with. After that, I just can't say what they've been up to. No offense, your servants are going to wonder what *we're* up to in here if I don't show them some lamplight under yonder door."

She languidly replied, "They've retired to their own quarters in the back, if they know what's good for them. I like a man who gets down to brass tacks without shilly-shally."

Longarm didn't answer. Her tone was colder as she quietly asked him, "Has the cat got your tongue? Why don't you say something, or better yet, *do* something? I know I've put on a little weight, but I guess I can keep up with that miner's widow you've been taking to the opera down in Denver this season!"

Longarm took a deep breath, let half of it out so he'd have his voice reined in tight, and said, "Let's get one thing straight right off, Miss Flora. I don't talk about ladies I might or might not take to the opera. How would you like it if I . . . took you to the opera and then told everybody how swell you . . . sang?"

She leaned toward him in the dark to softly but insistently say, "I don't know. Why don't you throw me down and make me sing?"

Chapter 15

Longarm figured he was damned if he did and damned if he didn't, so he did, and it sure beat all how a gal with a well-rounded rump presented her privates at just the right angle on a firm foundation. But lest they wind up with rug burns, they waited until they were up in her four-poster in a right romantic tower room before they took their duds off entirely.

He felt better about the whole deal with the one door bolted and the third-story windows offering such a wide field of fire three ways out and down. Flora confessed she often spent the night up there bare-ass atop the bedding. "Up among the stars," as she put it.

He didn't ask if she'd invited him up yonder because she'd heard so much about him being a ladies' man, or because she'd heard a lawman couldn't arrest a lady he'd been up among the stars with.

Both views were a bit oversimplified. Like a lot of modest gents had found out ahead of him, others tended to credit you with far more conquests than were humanly possible when you just smiled and offered no brags of your own while others droned on about their bedroom exploits.

The notion that a lawman couldn't arrest a suspect he'd

been screwing had occasioned many a false accusation and a few mighty friendly investigations. It was true the lawyer of the accused could and often would make it awkward in court for an arresting officer who'd enjoyed the favors of the lady on trial. It was also true that on more than one occasion Longarm had cracked a case while caressing the crack of one who knew more than she'd been letting on.

So as they floated in her four-poster among the stars, in some of the damnedest positions, Longarm took Flora step by step over the whole case, from the wire pulling him off another case, to her rental agent riding off on that thoroughbred.

Flora confided, dog-style, that her uncle, Red Jim Elliot, had taken Frazer on as his *segundo* while she'd been at school back East. She said her uncle had adopted her as his heiress when her mother, his kid sister, had died in Nova Scotia not long after his wife had passed away childless out Colorado way.

When he asked if that made her and her uncle Canadians too, she pointed out that Nova Scotia was a long way from the Red River of the north, and asked, "Do you suspect the famous Bat Masterson and that poor lawyer McSween you were talking about of being Canadian rebels, seeing both of them hailed from Canada, the same as Louis Riel?"

Longarm said, "Not hardly. But your uncle being from Canada to begin with would account for him hiring another Canadian as his rental agent, and it's commencing to look as if the common denominator is Canadian background, not Canadian rebel tendencies. Mix a whole lot of mean Canadians together, and you're fixing to get all sorts of mean Canadians from Red River Breeds to Scotchmen from Nova Scotia. Let's turn you over and finish right."

She moaned that she wanted him to hit bottom with every stroke, and it sure was fun to try. After they'd come that way and paused for a shared smoke, Flora asked him what the meaning of it all might be.

He got a cheroot going and confessed, "I don't know for certain, but I'm commencing to see a hazy pattern. Sister Simone was packing a whole lot of loot when they stopped her at the border. They think it was from a bank robbery up Canada way. It might have been. They might have come by it some other way. The point is that she was on her way south with it. At the same time, other Canadian wants have been gathering down this way in numbers, to do something big. When Sister Simone told that corrupt and horny constable he could be in on it, he threw over his job and abandoned his homestead to head down this way after covering his tracks first. They've all been covering their tracks a heap. Moving from one hideout to another to make sure nobody's on to them."

"I meant what's the meaning of all *this* that we've been doing!" she demanded, being a woman in bed with a man.

He sighed and said, "The meaning of a man with a maid in a bed is that it feels way better than pissing. I'm talking about a *serious* mystery, honey lamb."

She said she was sorry and snuggled closer, asking him to tell her more.

He said, "There ain't much more. They're fixing to pull something off. Something big that calls for money and muscle. It has to be simple in plan. Tom Frazer had a head for figures, I reckon. But some of the others mixed up in this can best be described as half-cracked and totally impulsive."

"Isn't there a U.S. Mint in Denver?" she suggested.

He tweaked a tit and said, "Don't laugh. It's got to be something they just don't have to rob up Canada way. So what might we have to offer them that they don't have up yonder?"

She said she didn't know, and asked if she could get on top, seeing he only wanted to puff and mutter.

He let her, and that sure beat pissing as well, for she was able to move her considerable charms with surprising grace for what it all had to weigh.

But even as she tried to take his mind off such stuffy things as banks, railroads, stage lines, and so on, he found himself drifting back to them. They had all such things to rob in Canada, and come to study on it, Fort Collins, Cheyenne, and the gold fields of Montana between!

The university across town? They had a college up to Collins if the intent was to get educated at gunpoint. So what in blue blazes was down this way for such a sneaky bunch to be after?

He never figured it out that night, and come morning, he was served breakfast in bed by an Indian gal in a French maid's uniform who told him Madam was having her ham and eggs with a bubble bath next door.

There was a lot to be said for being so rich, he decided, as he reclined under satin sheets with a tray of grand grub and a high and wide view of the whole town spread out below as if for his inspection. The silver plate and jewelry Tom Frazer could have stolen at this one address alone made Longarm wonder what in thunder Frazer and the others could be out to steal instead.

They had to be out to steal *something*. Nobody recruited a small army of hardcase hairpins, whores, and hired guns to set up a toy factory.

He was still mulling it over in his mind an hour later at the Western Union, where he'd gone to send his own progress report, leaving out a few juicy details.

As he came out, he met up with Crown Sergeant Foster, who'd picked up his own undertaker's outfit at that same tailor, seeing there was no point in looking like a pair of hayseeds now that everyone in Boulder who mattered knew they were there.

Foster said, "I was hoping you'd be here. I was just about to wire that I couldn't find you and might have to go on alone."

"Go on alone where?" asked Longarm.

Foster said, "Cheyenne. They just found Tom Frazer. He must have ridden that fast horse a short ways and caught a northbound late last night."

Longarm thought and decided, "That works. Where are they holding him for us?"

The Mountie said, "The city morgue. Seems they found him bound hand and foot and full of lead on some construction site up there. I understand there's an afternoon train we can catch to Cheyenne."

Longarm said, "Burlington combination. Catching it ain't the problem. Whether we *want* to catch it or not is the problem. What if they just left his body to be found there to get us out of Boulder?"

Foster shrugged and said, "What if the dog hadn't stopped to shit? The rabbit would still be in Cheyenne! We've *flushed* the game down this way, Long. To have killed a Boulder rental agent in Cheyenne, some killer from Colorado must have followed him up to Wyoming Territory!"

"Or rid the train up with him like a pal." Longarm nodded, then decided, "When you're right you're right. LeClerc upset their apple cart here in Boulder by getting his fool self shot. That gal who shot him knew it was time to just cut and run. Tom Frazer made the mistake of trying to tidy up and telling somebody where he was running."

"Cheyenne being on the way home to Canada," the Canadian Mountie agreed.

So Longarm didn't like it, but like or lump it, the trail of Tom Frazer and at least one other member of the gang led to Cheyenne, and nothing he could dig up in Boulder seemed to lead anywhere, so what the hell.

They got into Cheyenne that evening, and having read the wires from there more than once aboard the train, headed directly for the murder site, just a couple of blocks west of the railroad station on Lincolnway..

There were still some Cheyenne copper badges policing the construction site when Longarm and the Mountie ambled over. They were told the pile of cast-iron Roman columns and buttresses piled back closer to the railroad yards to the south was going to be the new Hoffman Building, Cheyenne's answer to the cast-iron facades of Chicago Town. The body of Tom Frazer had been dumped in the partly flooded lower depths of the proposed basement, dug down through prairie loam to the water table.

Longarm opined, "There was more than one killer. They overpowered him and tied him up over in them railroad yards. Then they carried him around that pile of cast-iron facade elements to pump him full of lead. Let's go have a look at him."

They did. It wasn't far. Most everything in Cheyenne was within a furlong of Central Avenue and Lincolnway, with "Uncle Pete" or the Union Pacific Railroad the most important business in town.

Longarm had never seen the hatchet-faced cuss staring up at the overhead lamp from a zinc-topped table before. But Crown Sergeant Foster had. So even though the papers in his wallet still said he was Thomas Frazer of Boulder County, the Mounties had him down as one Martin Quinn, wanted in Moose Jaw for embezzlement.

Foster said that four or five years back the man on the zinc table had lit out with the contents of a cash till left in his care. Foster said, "He'd told some friends in Moose Jaw he was headed to BC for a new start. I suppose he meant Boulder, Colorado, instead of British Columbia, eh, what?"

Longarm replied, "I reckon so. But how much did he steal up your way, and what do you reckon he was out to steal down our way?"

Foster said, "A little over nine thousand Canadian, of course. It wasn't the amount so much as the violated trust that outraged everyone in Moose Jaw. He was more a petty thief than a desperado, and you say he'd been working for that Elliot estate, entrusted with all that rent money, month after month?"

Longarm soberly replied, "Makes you wonder, don't it? He could have lit out any time with more than nine thousand American. So he must've been playing for higher stakes. Sister Simone or the jaspers riding down from Canada with her had some money to ante up. I'd say we had a serious Canadian crook masterminding something serious as all get-out, not up *your* way but down *mine*!"

Foster didn't argue that point. He decided, "Quinn here doesn't work as your mastermind. The mastermind ordered him killed to keep him from talking when they saw we were closing in. So who would have noticed us closing in on this particular target?"

Longarm grimaced and said, "I could list 'em numerical or by the alphabet. The gang was using property he managed as a recruiting center. Once the DuPrix woman blew away a recruit or a sucker in the Flatiron Hotel, it was only a question of time before we canvased our way to the rental office he was working in as Tom Frazer. So, like the DuPrix woman, he ran for it. He was likely headed back to Canada. He would have changed trains here, if they hadn't stopped him."

Foster griped, "Then canvasing the transient hotels along that Lincolnway is probably a total waste of time, eh, what?"

Longarm shrugged and suggested, "It ain't like we have better things to do. The night is young and we may get lucky. On the outside chance he meant to head east or west to the bright lights of Omaha of Frisco, he'd have had to wait here overnight for a transcontinental going either way."

So they thanked the Wyoming lawmen and allowed they'd snoop about on their own for a spell.

The spell lasted quite a while. There were lots of hotels and ten times that many saloons along Lincolnway, which ran east and west in line with Uncle Pete's rail yards.

Most of the rails and sidings ran east and west the same way. But feeder lines from the north and south, such as the Burlington spur they'd come up on, tended to cut across the busy Lincolnway directly, or at odd angles because of the way the tracks had to circle around from north or south to east or west. One such cloverleaf was occupied by a ragged-ass row of cheap hotels, honky-tonk saloons, and a back row of crib houses catering to railroad workers and cowhands off the surrounding range. So the two more sedately dressed strangers caught some withering looks as they entered in search of some suds and information.

As the barkeep warily served them, a brogue down the bar you could cut with a knife muttered, "Sure and ain't we the fine English gentry, dispensing goodwill amid the tenants this gracious good night!"

So Longarm and Foster believed the barkeep when he allowed they didn't serve many out-of-towners there.

Knowing from earlier visits they were headed into darker and less settled parts, Longarm was about to suggest they head back the other way when he heard the not-too-dulcet sounds of a piano in dire need of a tuning or a pianist in dire need of piano lessons.

Longarm brightened and said, "I think we're in luck. I only know one saloon pianist who plays like that, and she's played requests for just about every knock-around-hairpin west of the Big Muddy! Come on. I'll ask her if she has a friend for you!"

Red Robin, as the junoesque gal pounding an upright in a scarlet velveteen dress under a mop of henna-red hair was known, told Longarm she'd think about that while she finished her set. Meanwhile, she was being threatened with dismissal for flirting on the job. So Longarm and Foster found a corner table and ordered hard liquor with their pitcher of suds to show they were spenders. Then they nursed all the liquid while Red Robin played on, and on, as only saloon players can when they play that poorly. Red Robin got by on her looks and friendly attitude towards men. She still had to move on more than most.

During her break Red Robin joined them, shook friendly with Foster, and allowed that her pal Nicole, that chestnut-haired barmaid, might go along with them.

She talked to the other gal on her way back to her piano. From the thoughful glances they got while Red Robin played on, and on, Longarm figured Foster was going to wind up owing him.

But during her next break, Red Robin asked Longarm if they could have a word in private. When he rose to step away from the table with her, Red Robin demurely whispered, "Custis, we've known one another through thick and thin and dog style. So would you take it wrong if I asked for something more unusual tonight?"

Longarm smiled down at her and gallantly replied, "I was looking forward to more dog style. But if you'd like to swap, I'll just have to be a good sport about it."

Chapter 16

"Aren't you the least bit jealous?" asked Nicole as they shared a smoke atop her covers to cool their naked, fevered flesh after a ride down the primrose path to remember. He could see enough of what he was cuddled up with by the street glow through her lace curtains to truthfully reply, "Red Robin and me go back a ways and it's always been grand, but variety is the spice of life, and one thing that the two of us have in common is a natural curiosity about life."

The taller, more slender Nicole chuckled sort of dirty and confessed, "Had I wound up with that husky Canadian I'd have wound up wondering what I'd missed with you. How am I different from that new piano gal, aside from being younger, I mean?"

Longarm soberly told her, "Don't be catty about a pal who fixed you up to get fucked, girl. Red Robin is a friend of mine and I reckon, if the truth be known, I'd have preferred to fuck the two of you and leave any other men out of it."

She said, "I'm sorry, and that sounds like fun. Maybe later, after he goes back to Canada. But seriously, how come you wanted me instead of her tonight, if you like her so much?"

Longarm answered simply, "Why do happily married men frequent houses of ill repute? I'm a man. Men have always wanted to know what was over the hill or up a skirt. Doc Darwin says it's a good thing. Our ancestors would have frozen to death during a spell of cold weather way back when, and none of us would be here, if men hadn't been curious enough to explore their world to where they knew the best shelters and hunting grounds."

"Then that's all I am to you, a strange piece of ass?" Nicole asked in a hurt tone.

He said, "Nope. I was interested in your mind."

The chestnut-headed and pubic-haired barmaid snapped, "You don't have to be insulting, you smug bastard! I swear, you tell some men they have a lovely cock and they think they can walk all over you!"

Longarm patted her bare shoulder and put out the smoke to grab for some ass as he said soothingly, "I mean it. I don't mean I wanted you to teach me how to mix drinks. I wanted to talk to you about the drunks you've been serving of late."

She calmed down, and seemed interested as he felt her up and filled her in on the field mission he was on. Taking hold of his wrist to guide his hand further down, the gal told him she'd heard talk about a gathering of the Canadian clans, Scotch as well as French Canuck. That added up to country boys of the Canadian West. It seemed most every early trapper and Indian trader who hadn't been French had been Scotch, and they'd both screwed all the Indians they could get to hold still long enough.

Nicole said she didn't have any details to offer because a barmaid had to keep moving up and down the mahogany, and hardcases with real secrets tended to clam up while they were being served.

But she had picked up enough in bits and pieces to hazard a guess that Sister Simone's gang had sent for outside help, a lot of outside help, and that big money, a lot of big money, had been promised for one and all at the end of the rainbow, somewhere down the Front Range.

Longarm commenced to strum her old banjo as he nuzzled her earlobe and murmured, "Don't matter whether the ones behind all this intend to pay off or not. That many owlhoot riders congregating just north of Denver adds up to a whole lot of trouble for somebody just north of Denver, and that cavalry post, Camp Weld, lies *south* of Denver!"

"Oh, Custis, you talk so romantic when you finger-fuck a lady!" the lady he was finger-fucking moaned. So he kissed her lips instead of her fool earlobe, and rolled between her welcoming thighs to fuck her right.

It was easy. The trim Nicole was well legged-up from working on her feet twelve hours a day, and once a man was in her love saddle with his manhood firmly rooted through that chestnut thatch, he just had to *stay* in the saddle and let her buck!

It was tempting to repeat what Red Robin had said about dog style as they tried it that way too. But he just enjoyed the contrasting view as he stared down at his old organ-grinder sliding in and out to meet slimmer hips and firmer buttocks. He wondered if Red Robin was comparing his body with Foster's right this moment, as the both of them enjoyed the variety as much as the ins and outs. They'd both agreed on more intimate occasions that nobody else they knew did it any better, while a lot of folks you met up with didn't do it half so well. But as some kindly old philosopher had once remarked, no doubt in French, nine out of ten folks were worth fucking, and that tenth bad fuck was a break in the monotony. So Longarm and Red Robin had decided to meet now and then with no promises and keep one another out of trouble.

When Nicole, face crushed in the pillows and rump upthrust to take it deeper, asked how long he meant to be in Cheyenne, Longarm reminded himself that, grand as she upthrust, Red Robin, that widow on Sherman Street, and a gunslinging blonde down Texas way all offered the same inducements but didn't demand a man stick around.

So he told her he doubted they'd be there long, seeing the Canadian crook they knew of in town lay dead in the morgue at the moment.

So seeing she'd never have to face him at work, once she calmed down, Nicole allowed there was this experiment she'd always wanted to try if a swain would promise to stop if she didn't like it.

She didn't like it. So Longarm stopped. As she got on top the old-fashioned way to make it up to him, Longarm asked, "Do you reckon you might kill a man if he wanted to do something that hurt and you just didn't want him to?"

Nicole said, "I don't think I'd kill him. It didn't feel *that* bad. But I guess I'd never speak to him again. Why do you ask?"

He said he was thinking about a gal who'd picked up a man on a college campus and never spoke to him again.

There was no sense asking a gal who hadn't been there whether she thought Constable LeClerc had been led astray by promises of filthy lucre, dirty sex, or both. She told him later that although she'd heard lots of dirty stories about nuns and priests, she took them with a grain of salt and wasn't certain Sister Simone was a real person.

She said, "Some mining men from over in the Black Hills were talking about that Deadwood Dick one night. One said he'd had a drink with the one and original Deadwood Dick in the Number Ten Saloon. But yet another Deadwood man said Deadwood Dick was a made-up range detective in an English magazine published in London Town."

Longarm said, "They were both as right or wrong.

Deadwood Dick first strides the pages of history in a penny dreadful magazine. But since then at least three flesh-and-blood imbibers of strong spirits have come forward swearing to the title and ready to fight anybody smaller who says it isn't so."

He chuckled fondly as he recalled that Texas hand of the African persuasion who modestly explained he'd won the nickname by winning the first riding and roping contest held in Deadwood, back in '76. Had Nate Love ever been to Deadwood, he'd have noticed it was a mining camp with little or no interest in such skills, back in the year they first struck color in Deadwood Gulch or any time since.

He decided, "Sister Simone *would* work better as a hard-riding hard-drinking bawd—like that crazy Bell Starr over to Younger's Bend—who took to calling herself Sister Simone after the legends inspired by a French postcard."

Nicole laughed and said he was a naughty boy if he'd been jacking off over the set of postcards she and the other gals had been showing one another on the sly.

Nicole said, "This Irish girl at work says some bad girls just dressed up as nuns to make those poses seem more shocking. She said both those bad girls and the photographer must have been dirty-minded Protestants who didn't know any better."

"She could tell by the habits they were wearing, or the habits they weren't really covering much with?" Longarm asked.

Nicole said, "I don't know how she could tell. You'd have to ask her!"

So Longarm allowed he would, and asked who that Irish gal was and how he might get in touch with her.

The chestnut-haired Protestant gal said, "You want Angela, working the day shift, starting at noon. You don't want to go to her quarters over in Shanty Town. Her father is ashamed to have a daughter working in a saloon. But *somebody* in the family had to find regular work when he was fired by Uncle Pete for drinking in the signal tower. Red Robin and me sleep late and report for work near the end of her shift. So stick with me, baby, and I'll fix you up with a gal who won't put out in a million years!"

It would have been a waste of time to assure Nicole he didn't want to get sassy with that other barmaid. To begin with, he hadn't seen her yet.

But he and Crown Sergeant Foster had agreed to meet for breakfast and a strategy meeting across from the Western Union come morning, and he didn't want to wait half the day to find out how you might tell a real nun from a fake nun in a dirty group tintype.

Being a lighter sleeper than the hard-worked and thoroughly screwed Nicole, Longarm was awakened early by the distant wistful moan of a locomotive approaching a crossing. Longarm was now well traveled to where he followed the drift of railroad signals. But when it caught him by surprise, that haunting sound in the distance called the kid in him to run off to strange places with names like Camelot or Timbuktu.

That cold gray morning he just slid out from under the covers, and when Nicole murmured in her sleep, he patted her bare tit until she muttered, "Not now, damn it, I'm sleepy!"

That seemed to work every time. He gathered up his duds and dressed out on the stair landing in the semi-darkness. There was no graceful way to pound on the door of Red Robin's hotel room to ask if Foster was up. So he eased on down the stairs, trying not to picture Red Robin being so kind to another man by the dawn's early light.

The two lawmen had naturally left their saddles and such at the station baggage room while they made up their minds about their stay in Cheyenne.

It hardly seemed likely the killers had put down roots

after shooting Tom Frazer or Martin Quinn so close to the station. Foster knew what the infamous Sister Simone looked like. Longarm had yet to see that one postcard, let alone a whole set. It was too early to scout up that Irish gal of Papist persuasion. But once they could, Foster might or might not recall some detail real nuns being dirty might have included. Longarm knew how easy it was for someone playing let's pretend to slip up while posing in costume. He still chuckled every time he recalled that famous Indian fighter posing for the newspaper artists in those fancy fringed buckskins, beaded fit to bust with dyed porcupine quills, declaring their wearer a grandmother with powers of divination.

He got to the Western Union, slipped inside to get off a progress report to Denver, and headed across to the beanery. Foster wasn't there yet, the horny son of a bitch. Longarm sat at the counter and ordered coffee and donuts to start, explaining to the waitress behind the counter that he and a slugabed pal would be eating more seriously at one of their tables as soon as he got there.

Then, seeing the place was empty and he hadn't had a chance to wash up at that seedy hotel up the way, he left his stool at the counter to thread his way through the bare tables scattered across the tile floor to a door marked *Gentlemen*.

Gentlemen were supposed to heed the call to nature in a shed to one side of the back door. Ladies got to crap in the other one. But there was a sink with running water and a mirror just inside that first door marked *Gentlemen*. So Longarm spent some time cleaning up, and when he stepped back out, his coffee and donuts were waiting for him on the counter. A nicely built brunette with cameo features and red-rimmed eyes was seated there as well.

He didn't care, and there was no proper way for a gentleman to ask a lady he'd never been introduced to what she was crying about. So he just nodded and reached for a donut as she softly asked if he was a lawman, as they'd told her at the Western Union across the way.

He nodded again and pled guilty, hoping she wasn't going to ask him to look for a lost pup. She seemed to have her purse intact in the lap of her dark gray travel duster.

She looked around as if afraid she'd be overheard, and then she took a deep breath and said, "My name is Celine DuPrix and I seem to be in a lot of trouble!"

Longarm managed to get the lump of donut down without choking himself to death, although it wasn't easy, sipped some coffee to wet his whistle, and calmly replied, "You surely are, Miss Celine. No offense, but you ain't one of them Métis, are you?"

She said, "No. That Canadian rebel movement has nothing to do with the bigger mess I'm mixed up in. They've killed my husband, they mean to kill me. They want to kill me before I can tell all I know to the law! So tell me, what kind of a deal do you think I can make with the law about another little problem?"

Longarm soberly replied, "A charge of manslaughter at the least ain't a little problem, Miss Celine. But why don't you start at the beginning, and I'll see if I can figure out some way to save your neck at least."

She said they had to do better than that.

He shrugged and suggested they wait for her fellow Canadian, Crown Sergeant Foster, to explain local customs to her.

He waved his donut at the front window, adding, "He ought to be along any time now."

She followed his glance without thinking, flinched, and gasped, *"Mon Dieu!* I thought I had lost them! I hid all night in the ladies' room at the depot, but they must have known I was somewhere in this part of the city, *hein?"*

He followed her glance to see that sure enough a quartet of what could have been taken for cowhands in off the surrounding range were lined up along the walk across the way in desperately casual poses.

All four were wearing six-guns and packing saddle guns, as if they'd come in from a coyote hunt.

Celine DuPrix moaned, "They know I am in here! They must have had someone watching the *gare,* I mean depot. Let us flee out the back way before it is too late, *non?*"

To which Longarm grimly replied, "*Non,* it's already too late, Miss Celine. Them rascals across the way wouldn't be showing themselves so bold out front if they hadn't already covered the back."

Chapter 17

The waitress working the morning shift alone, a hefty gal who looked as if she could hold her own if she had to, was neither deaf nor made of clay. So she called for the cook in the back and told Longarm they kept a Harrington Richardson .36 under the cash till.

As the burly Greek cook joined them, Longarm declared, "I doubt they have the hair on their chests to move in on us at this hour in Downtown Cheyenne. We ain't but five or six city blocks from the Territorial Capitol grounds."

"I don't know. They're still out there," said the waitress. So Longarm didn't try to stop her as she moved down the counter to arm herself with that little whore pistol.

He steered Celine DuPrix to a corner table out of line with either the front or back doors, suggesting, "We'll fort up and wait them out. That Canadian Mountie I just mentioned will be along any minute and he has an eye for Canadian outlaws. Those *are* Canadian outlaws, right?"

She said she only recognized a couple as he helped her into the corner, taking her purse away and reaching in to haul out what was likely criminal evidence.

She stammered, "*Mais non*, that is my gun and those terrible men wish to murder me!"

He said, "Set yourself down and let me worry about them. I might as well tell you I saw what you did with this .32 to Constable LeClerc, and impulsive gals with guns set my teeth on edge."

She sobbed, "They will kill us both! You are outnumbered two to one and those men are *trés formidables!*"

"Tell me about Tom Frazer or Martin Quinn first," he suggested, adding, "Did I hear you right about him being your *husband*?"

When she nodded tearfully, and he opined it was a poor excuse for a man who'd send a wife on a whore's mission, she spilled that part of her story in a rush.

She, Celine Quinn née DuPrix of Montreal, had been recruited at the last moment when Sister Simone, who should have been there to meet Constable LeClerc, lit out of Fort Collins without ever coming back to Boulder. Quinn, in charge of sheltering and steering new recruits from one hideout to another, had figured Sister Simone had gotten spooked when her derby-hatted partner, Chambrun, had wound up so dead.

Longarm asked if Celine knew where that nunnery Sister Simone hid out in between rampages might be located.

She said she'd only met the wildwoman of the Canadian West a few times, never in a nun's habit or even her Cree buckskins. She went on to explain how they'd recruited her to traipse around the UC campus until it looked safe to approach the figure on that appointed bench, exchange passwords, and carry him over to the Flatiron Hotel. LeClerc had got his fool self killed the old-fashioned way some horny souls forgot to watch out for. The very devout young wife of an unabashed crook had simply said no and defended her honor with a .32.

He asked what the password had been. She explained there hadn't been a formal code. She'd been recruited to

143

pick LeClerc up because they both spoke the Quebecois version of French. She said she hadn't been willing, and LeClerc had scared her skinny by treating her like the whore he'd doubtless taken her for.

Longarm said, "His mistake might have been our gain. Boulder County and me might buy a defense of a lady's honor if you can convince us you're a lady. Do you have much of a record of your own, before you took to shooting constables, I mean?"

She sobbed, "Perhaps a *soupçon* of the shoplifting. One time this, how you say, badger game that caused no loss of the blood. But that *corps diabolique* my poor Martin was lured into—"

"You're going to have to talk English if you want me to follow your drift," he cut in. "How can you say your man was sucked in when he was one of the recruiters, and what in blue thunder did he and the leadership *want* with so many armed and dangerous Canadians?"

From the counter their waitress called, "The street out front is starting to crowd up with others on their way to work, and I don't see those rough-looking riders now!"

Longarm wanted to shoot her. Before her words could sink in, he warned the recently widowed Celine Quinn, "You're going to have to give us more than a sad story, ma'am. Who put the master plan together and what was the master plan? You were saying your man was storing away hardcase Canucks like acorns for the winter when things went to Hell in a hack. I see now that your man slickered his pals by hiding you out as that Denver-bound local left Boulder. Then the two of you ran up this way and . . . how did they get him?"

She answered simply, "We arrived, we thought, undetected. We were waiting for our connection to California when my poor Martin he tells me to run into the ladies' room *tout de suite*. He runs some other way. That is all I know until I learn much later the police find my poor Martin has been murdered. It is not as difficult to, how you say, hide out in a ladies' room for the very long time, as long as you have the cash to send attendants out to make *tres* discreet purchases and inquiries. When I think they have given up, and hear at the Western Union how the famous Longarm has just left to come in here for breakfast—"

"Who were you out to wire?" he cut in.

She looked surprised and replied, "*Ma famille* in Montreal, of course. Why would I want to go on to California without my poor Martin? It was he who, how you say, took *le premier pas* leading us deeper and deeper into all this trouble in a strange land, *non*?"

Longarm said, "*Non*. I just told you how much trouble you got into all by yourself, no offense. Get to the good part. What is that swamping gang planning to pull off down here in my jurisdiction?"

He wanted to shoot Crown Sergeant Foster when the burly Mountie barged in to exclaim, "Sorry I'm late. Just recognized another want on the street out front. Chased the blighter two blocks before I lost him behind a hay wain stalled in the traffic."

Longarm said, "You missed three more out front and at least two laying for us out back."

He introduced Celine Quinn née DuPrix, and filled the Mountie in faster than she could have, since he spoke plain English.

Foster chortled, "I say, the best-laid plans of mice, men, and Sister Simone seem to have gone aglae over a simple misunderstanding and now they're all running back to Canada!"

Longarm stared thoughtfully at the petite brunette LeClerc had taken for as bawdy a strumpet as Sister Simone, and decided, "Mebbe. It's as likely the slick planner who put this whole game together had this lady's husband killed, and wants her dead lest she tell us what the plan might be."

He frowned sternly at the young Widow Quinn and

pointed out, "The sooner you tell us what the plan is, the less good it will do them to kill you, Miss Celine. Can't you see that if they're as smart as you seem to fear, they'd be dumb to risk killing you for no good reason?"

She insisted Tom Frazer or Martin Quinn hadn't confided the whole plan to her, assuming he'd *known* the whole plan. She said he'd sent for her once he'd gotten a new start down Colorado way as an honest rental agent for that gruff but kindly fellow Canadian Red Jim Elliot. She said she thought someone had led her poor *gobemouches* down the path to perdition after Red Jim had upped and died on them, leaving her poor Martin unsupervised as he fell in with bad company collecting rents in rotgut saloons and houses of ill repute. Foster quietly explained a *gobemouches* was a fly swallower or total sucker. Longarm said he didn't care, and asked if she thought Quinn's new boss, Miss Flora, had a direct interest in any of the whorehouses she rented her property out to.

Celine Quinn said she'd never met Flora Bell and didn't know. He advised her to think harder.

A couple of copper badges came in to tell Foster they were watching the depot and public liveries. That was the first Longarm knew about Foster having sent a roundsman for help after losing the well-known Ace Lancing of Alberta in the morning rush. Foster introduced everybody. The Cheyenne lawmen allowed they'd heard of Longarm and were pleased as punch to be working with him.

When they asked what they were working on with him, Longarm asked if they'd take Celine Quinn née DuPrix over to their lockup and hold her pending extradition proceedings.

Foster seemed to think Longarm meant extradition to Canada, until Longarm explained, "Not hardly. She may be a British subject and she may have filled a British subject full of lead. But she did it in Colorado, which is where they're going to want to hold her trial."

The Canadian Mountie started to object before Longarm added, "She may or may not have some friends or relations coming forward to see if they can bail her out, hire her a good defense team, or whatever."

Then Foster said, "Oh, I say," and said nothing more about it.

As the Cheyenne lawmen asked her politely to come along with them, Celine shot Longarm an imploring look. He said, "If you send for me and I'm in the same town, I'll come see what you have to say. If I ain't in town, I won't. If you send for me and don't have anything new to tell me, I'll be mighty cross with you and I'll say that to the judge when, not if, they call me as a witness."

As they led her away, Foster opined, "I don't think she's going to break. Why should she? She has nothing to gain and a lot to lose if she admits to criminal conspiracy on top of justifiable homicide."

Longarm said, "Worse yet, she could be telling the truth. I hate it when they do that!"

The Mountie sighed and said, "Quinn proved she was flighty when he sent her to pick up LeClerc with a gun in her purse. He could have been keeping her in the dark, and only asked her to play a small part in the game when that Sister Simone threw a wrench in the machinery by running back to her nunnery. I've wired Fort MacLeod to canvas all the teaching missions west of Ottawa about recent sabbaticals. But we've been over that ground before without much luck. The infernal bead-mumbling Frogs don't seem to want to talk to us for some damned reason."

Longarm said, "Let's eat. We've plenty of time. Then, while you and the copper badges hunt for those Canadian gunslicks, I'm fixing to drop by for a visit with an Irish barmaid of the Papist persuasion. I might be able to get more out of her if I don't call her a bead-mumbling harp, as gents who row for Harrow might put it."

147

So an hour later the blond Angela O'Connor, descended from the Royal O'Connors but forced into service by the perfidious Saxons, was happy to see a customer that early in the day, and didn't get mad when he flashed his badge after paying for his drink.

They were alone in the fair-sized saloon at that hour, save for a swamper spreading fresh sawdust on the floor and a regular down the bar talking to his beer schooner. So Longarm leaned closer to confide he was there as an officer of the law on a matter of some delicacy. Herself leaned close from her side of the mock mahogany to ask whose moral lapses they were talking about and all.

Longarm said, "It's my understanding you said that you could tell a real nun from another sort of gal entirely, pretending to be a nun acting dirty in a nunnery."

The big blonde blushed and looked away, stammering, "I never bought them postcards myself, and the boy who was selling them on the sly was fired by Himself, who runs a decent place here!"

Longarm nodded and said, "That's what I heard. I heard you were the one who exposed those naughty postcards as posed pornography by gals just pretending to be nuns. So tell me, what gave the show away?"

She replied, "Sure that was easy. None of them was wearing rings."

"Real nuns are supposed to wear rings?" Longarm asked, trying to think back.

Angela O'Connor sounded certain as she explained, "They are, for ain't they the brides of Christ and wouldn't you expect them to be after wearing wedding rings?"

As a matter of fact, he hadn't. But the notion made sense as soon as you studied on it. He insisted, "You're certain none of the naughty gals posing for them postcards wore proper wedding rings?"

She insisted, "Them pictures weren't naughty. They was filthy, and the three of them sacrilegious bawds will burn in Hell forever after working to discredit the Faith

148

like that. And why do you suppose even a lost soul would want to dress up like a nun before posing in such uncomfortable and dirty positions?"

Longarm said, "To make the pictures seem more shocking if they were staged in some studio with fake costumes. But I've been assured at least one of those . . . models is known as Sister Simone and she was overheard saying she had to get back to her nunnery."

The Irish girl shook her head and insisted, "A bawd who'd lie like that would no doubt be the one so fond of that bottle! I don't care what she said about belonging in a convent. If she was a real nun she'd be after wearing her ring, wouldn't she?"

He started to nod. Then he mused half to himself, "Some married-up gals who cheat on mortal husbands take their rings off in bed with the other man, out of respect for one or the other or both. Why would a gal tell a member of her gang she had to get back to her nunnery if she wasn't a nun?"

The Irish girl asked, "Sure what kind of a nun runs with a *gang* then? Is this some sort of nasty Protestant joke?"

He assured her, "If Sister Simone is what she says she is, she's the one playing nasty jokes on everybody, Miss Angela."

She declared that in that case the next drink was on the house and she got off at sundown.

But Longarm wasn't in Cheyenne at sundown. He was on his way south on the Burlington day-tripper after one hell of a row with the pride of the RCMP.

For Crown Sergeant Foster's position was that the gang of Canadian hardcases had fallen apart, whatever they'd been up to, and that he and his fellow Mounties were never going to enjoy such a duck hunt as a sudden mass migration of foiled villains was likely to present for the next few weeks.

Longarm's position was that he was buying no such

149

notion until such time as he knew what in blue blazes all those crazy Canucks had had in mind.

After recruiting far and wide for British subjects and only British subjects to gather in and about Boulder, they'd gone to great lengths to convince everyone the action was going to take place up the Front Range around Fort Collins. And, as he'd argued in vain with the burly Crown Sergeant Foster, the plan had been afoot far longer than Foster and others seemed ready to assume. Unless he was missing something, that robbery and murder of Gustav Persson and the fatal card game designed to frame Jacques Cartier in Fort Collins had taken place long before the recent flurry of hell-raising by Sister Simone. She and some of her gang had been raising hell along the Front Range soon after, if not sooner than, Tom Frazer or Martin Quinn had been on the scene. So Foster's idea that some Canadian crooks had thrown together some hasty scheme that had just blown up in their faces didn't sound right to Longarm. Some mighty slick mastermind had been waiting, and waiting, fixing to strike with a private army of infernal foreigners when, not before, the time was ripe!

Chapter 18

When he got back to Boulder, he discovered they hadn't heard from Wyoming about the extradition of Celine Quinn née DuPrix and that Flora Bell still liked him. That was more than could be said for that same snooty butler, who ushered Longarm into the drawing room as if he'd shown up with shit on his boots instead of a bunch of daisies, for Pete's sake.

Flora had other help put the daisies in a jar of water and fetch them to that tower room. Where she assured Longarm that since daisies wouldn't tell, they were safe with their own little secrets behind a bolted tower door.

After he got some kinks from his train ride out of his back with the assistance of his pleasantly plump hostess, he told her what had been going on and explained how his boss, the cantankerous Marshal Billy Vail, shared the opinion of Crown Sergeant Foster about further pursuit of the case.

When she asked him what he thought her murdered rental agent and all those strangers from Canada had been up to, he honestly confessed he just plain didn't know.

He added with a sigh, "Like Foster and my boss agree, we may never know now. We don't know how many of them there were in Boulder at one time. Such offenses as can be laid at Canadian feet seem to have been breaches of discipline, not meant as part of the master plan. If you recruit rough riders with long arrest records from either side of the border, you're bound to have some hell-raising in the ranks. Pawning a dead man's spurs and shooting folks in Fort Collins seems to have been designed to draw attention from some slipups this far south. Lord knows what ever happened to the frisky lads who robbed that rich stockman out of season. If the gal known down this way as Sister Simone was the same one the Mounties had down as inciting to riot and armed robbery up *their* way, she seems to have acted as a sort of currier cum con artist down *this* way. I was still working on her when Billy Vail wired for me to pack it in and come on home from Cheyenne."

She said she was so glad he'd dropped by on his way back to Denver. As they held hands and other parts atop the covers, she sighed and said, "In a way I wish someone would stop a train or rob a bank up this way, Custis. Do you think any of the bunch could still be left here in Boulder County?"

He assured her, "Not hiding out on your property. The county made sure of that whilst I was still up in Cheyenne. They've been hunting high and low for witnesses for and against Celine Quinn."

"She still refuses to talk?" asked the naked lady he was feeling up a tad faster now.

Longarm suggested, "She may not know more than she'd already told us. Let's finish dog-style lest I miss my train, no offense."

She laughed dirty, told him he was incorrigible, and rolled over to take it like a good sport. Dog style being the most conversationable position, and knowing he wouldn't be staying for supper, Flora asked him where she'd be able to find him the next time she went shopping down Denver way, if he wasn't going to chase Canadian crooks up her way anymore.

Humping steady with his feet planted on the rug by the side of the bed and a grand daylight view across the rooftops of Boulder, Longarm truthfully replied, "I ain't certain. They might send me back up into the uncertain country just west of the Divide. I was riding herd on a Land Management survey team, over by Shadow Mountain on recent Indian land, when that Canadian loot turning up in Fort Collins called me away. I don't know who they sent over the Divide to replace me. I hope they don't send me back. You've never minded children for a neighbor until you've played nursemaid to a pack of Eastern dudes in the high country in tick season!"

She moaned, "Faster, lover man! I'm almost there and, *Mon Dieu,* I hope they don't send you that far out in the field for a time!"

He sincerely said, "Me too!" as he humped her harder. "Them survey men know what they're about with their maps and fancy instruments, I reckon. But like I said, it's rough as well as unmapped country with hunters, trappers, and leftover Indians tending to cheat and steal from tenderfeet when they ain't giving them bum steers just to be funny."

She fell forward, moaning that she was coming, and he barely managed to keep it in with the same intent as he followed her down.

Before she could recover enough to ask for more, Longarm kissed her fondly, rolled off the bed, and got dressed without washing up while she called him an unfeeling brute.

That snooty butler didn't talk to Longarm as he showed him out. He likely listened at keyholes some, no matter what Flora said about her household help knowing their places in her scheme of things.

By the time he had his baggage checked through and boarded the local for the short ride to Denver, he was commencing to become more of a feeling brute than Flora had called him. It itched like hell when you put your pants on after screwing without wiping off your privates.

But fortunately, he was aboard one of those new Pullman coach cars, without the pull-down bunks but with fine sanitary facilities, for either sex, at either end. So he got up and eased forward to wash his recent sins away.

There was a fair-sized washroom with two side-by-side sinks under a grand mirror and a bench to their rear as if meant for an audience while others washed and shaved their faces or took down their pants. There was no way to take the towel roll into the crapping cubicle with him, but Longarm got out a clean pocket kerchief, rinsed it under a warm-water tap, and stepped into the awkward little crapper to shut the door, lower his tweed pants and knit-cotton underdrawers, and get tidied up down yonder with the damp kerchief before he took the time to let things dry some while he pissed on the railroad right of way.

You did that from a Pullman crapper because that was the way their up-to-date commodes flushed. There was a sign on the bulkhead by the pull chain, reading, "PLEASE DON'T FLUSH THE TOILET WHEN THE TRAIN IS STANDING IN THE STATION," because when you did, it left a mess next to the loading platform. As he stood there, holding the chain in one hand and his old organ-grinder in the other, Longarm could see railroad ties whipping by through the open brass trapdoor the swirling flush water was pouring out of. He let go of the chain after watering a furlong of dry ties and ballast, then hauled up his pants, adjusted his gun rig, and popped open the door unexpectedly as another cuss dressed for a funeral tore in to fire at his own reflection in the mirror and bust the glass all to hell.

Longarm drew and fired through the haze of gun smoke before the disoriented son of a bitch could figure out where his intended target was. Longarm knew he was the intended target. Who else might a cuss be intending to shoot when he follows one man alone into a shit house?

"Mais non, je suis hors de combat!" screamed his newfound playmate in a high agonized tone.

So Longarm snapped, "Speak English and toss that six-gun at my boots lest I horse your combination serious!"

As an RIC .455 British service revolver hit the swaying deck to slide into a far corner, the train conductor called in to say, "I'm waiting for some answers with the brakeman and a gun of my own!"

Longarm called back, "I'm U.S. Deputy Marshal Custis Long out of the Denver District Court. I don't know who I just shot. But I had to, and can you see if there's a doctor aboard this train?"

The smoke had thinned enough by then to make out the bent-over figure seated on that waiting-to-shave bench, holding his middle as he moaned and groaned in French.

Longarm repeated his command to speak English, adding, "You're in America now, and nobody invited all of you to come down here an' shoot the place up. I hope you can see that we've taken one of you alive at last. So I want you to listen tight. When I take you off this train in Denver, your role in this play is over and the only question in your mind should be your final paycheck. Before you tell me you're just an innocent young farmhand led astray, we both know you shoot fast and straight with intent to kill. Had I been in this compartment instead of the shittery just now, you'd have never chosen your own reflection as the only target in here. So you have to be a professional shootist with a record we can delve into as deep or shallow as the results may warrant. How do you like it so far?"

"This is not just!" the gutshot shootist moaned. "I waited until I was sure we would not be disturbed, and my gun she was in my hand when I came through the door! I should have won!"

Longarm got out a cheroot as he kept his six-gun trained and told the man he'd beat, "You didn't. So now the question before the house is whether you wind up in a prison cell or thirteen steps up with a loop of Kentucky hemp waiting there for you. A lot may depend on whether I tell the judge you were naughty or nice. It would be awfully nice of you to tell me what this is all about. Who sent all the way to Canada for you, and what other chores did he have in mind for you? I didn't know before yesterday I'd be boarding this train today, and I only decided a few minutes ago to wash up in here."

The badly wounded stranger moaned, "*Sacré* God damn, she burns like fire! She no say nothing about you, him, when I get the word in the Peace River country to the north of much money to be made down this way, *hein*? She still no tell me, him, just what I am to do when the coast is, how you say, clear. But many Quebecois have gather here in Colorado, along with Anglais and even Métis, chosen by one from the hills and plains of Alberta who has long been familiar with affairs of our *demi-monde*."

Longarm had enough French-speaking pals to know that that meant their underworld. He asked, "Was one of the job requirements hailing from Canada, or could other British subjects apply? How come your mastermind didn't invite any of our homegrown guns such as Frank and Jesse or the Kid to come along? I understand those three and others as handy with guns are looking for work after having their own gangs busted up by recent events. What were a bunch of riders apt to stand out in an American crowd supposed to do better than plain old owlhoots who know the country better?"

The conductor came in with a severe-looking woman packing a black oilcloth medical kit. She allowed she was a nurse, and asked the man Longarm had shot to let her take a look at his wound.

Longarm said, "I fired more than once, and he was about to tell me who he was, who he was riding for, and what he was doing in these parts before we do him any favors, ma'am."

She told him he was an unfeeling brute, and got the conductor to help her stretch the gutshot Canadian in black half open on the deck as he blubbered like a baby and swore at them in French.

The nurse commenced to cut his vest and shirt away as Longarm holstered his six-gun and hunkered down to address the man on the deck. He explained in a conversational tone, "I have to be true to my code. So I'll not go into detail, but not many folks in Boulder would have known I was passing through some more, and one of them, a lady who claims to be Scotch Canadian, spoke just a little French during a moment of excitement. So you and your pals have been riding for that Elliot estate and the man you all knew as Tom Frazer or Martin Quinn was just working for Miss Flora, right?"

"If you say so!" the obviously dying man moaned. "She no tell me more than she wants me to know, him."

Longarm growled, "Let's settle that one detail then. Have you been saying him or her? Is the mastermind a man or a woman—say, Miss Flora, or that mysterious Sister Simone who's been moving about like spit on a hot stove just out of sight?"

The man on his side didn't answer. The stern nurse told him why, her voice a little softer as she murmured, "He's unconscious. I don't expect him to come out of it. If he does he'll be able to tell you as much as your average vegetable."

"I never aimed for his *head*, ma'am," Longarm protested.

She said, "Drain enough blood from the brain and you may as well put a bullet through the same dead mush.

You nicked his aorta, from the way his belly's swollen. He'd been bleeding internally a lot. I don't see how he's going to make it to Denver General alive."

But he did. The gutshot rascal was pale as a ghost and cold as a clam with eyes as expressionless as Pacific oysters when they took him from the train. But he was still breathing, however shallowly, and at the hospital they told Longarm they could possibly save him with a delicate operation, and there was an outside chance he might even wake up again someday.

So Longarm went on over to the Denver Federal Building, where since it wasn't quite quitting time, he reported in to his boss, the somewhat older and far shorter and stouter Marshal Billy Vail.

News of the shooting aboard the train had preceded him. So his boss waited until Longarm had grabbed a seat across the cluttered desk in the oak-paneled inner office before he said, "You did as well as could be expected, old son. Betwixt the two of you, you and Foster busted the ring up and sent them packing. So what the hell."

Longarm lit a cheroot in self-defense because Billy Vail smoked what seemed to be dog turds and never opened his damned old windows.

As he shook out his match, Longarm mildly observed, "Forgive me for seeming such an old fuss, but I like to know what in blue blazes I was working on before I write my final report. Foster and me never busted up shit. There came a falling out amongst thieves, and whether they've busted up for good or not, I'd sure like to arrest the ringleader and ask what he, she, or it was planning for that private army of hardcase Canadians!"

Billy Vail calmly said, "You can't. There ain't enough evidence for an arrest and she'd only deny it."

Longarm blinked and demanded, "She? Are we talking about Sister Simone or Flora Bell, Boss?"

Vail said, "She spelt it LaBelle before she screwed Red

Jim Elliot and they told everybody she was his niece. I've been doing my own trailing on paper all this while. Like I said, we can't prove a thing in court. But it appears Red Jim, a Nova Scotian with a big appetite, had set the wheels in motion well before he came down with pneumonia last winter. His mistress and his *segundo*, Frazer-Quinn, have been trying to carry on without him, and as you saw, doing a piss-poor job!"

"Of what? What have they been planning?" Longarm almost wailed.

To which Vail calmly replied, "I have no idea."

Chapter 19

The older lawman shot an octopus screen of pungent blue smoke at Longarm and conceded, "I can hazard some educated guesses. But I'll be whipped with snakes if I can come up with a federal charge or even follow Red Jim Elliot's chain of reason as far as the time of his natural death."

Vail leaned back in his chair to continue. "I hate to say this, being of partly Scotch descent myself. But tight-fisted Scotchmen like Red Jim Elliot give Scots such as me and Silver Dollar Tabor a bad name. Red Jim was to true pioneers what buzzards are to wolves. They dine well with little effort after the wolves have brought down the game. The foothills of Boulder had been cleared of Arapaho and platted as an incorporated township before that Nova Scotian land pirate came swaggering in with his money belt and hired toughs to buy up or horn in on all that residential and business property at the beginning of the boom. He knew before he bullied his way to the feeding trough that the spanking-new state of Colorado was planning on building a state university yonder."

Longarm said, "That's the way you get rich in land speculation out this way. They told me Elliot had built some of his rental properties on land he'd no doubt begged, bought, or borrowed cheaper."

Vail shrugged and said, "Whatever. Suffice it to say, he died with a rep for horning in and helping himself to prime property. Where I lose the thread is the wilder bullshit since Red Jim passed the reins of his empire on to his play-pretty, named in his will as a niece. I asked Judge Dickerson down the hall about that. He says that since the will was never challenged in probate court, and since a dirty old man is allowed to call his common-law play-pretty anything he wants, nobody but a true son, daughter, or still-lawful widow would be in any position to contest her inheritance."

Longarm grimaced and decided, "So she's their leader, and all this time I thought she liked me for myself. But what in blue thunder has she been planning with all that extra help?"

Vail said, "I told you that was where I got stuck. In life, her so-called uncle and leader of the band got by with plenty of money and enough muscle to handle anyone who didn't enjoy doing business his way. She and Red Jim's late *segundo*, Frazer-Quinn, didn't need more than the handful of hardcases they already had on tap around Boulder."

"The original cadre was pure Canadian?" asked Longarm.

Vail said, "I reckon. Irish saloon keepers hire Irish barmaids. You seldom find an Irishman working as a cook for a Greek. So Red Jim Elliot was acting natural enough with a small core of mean Canucks. I just can't fathom what his survivors were fixing to do with a whole blamed cavalry troop of the same!"

Longarm said, "I see what you mean about having nothing to charge her with, even though I can't think of anyone else who might have had her rental agent killed for screwing up and ordering that clown on the train to . . . Now that's sort of odd as soon as you study on it!"

Vail asked what was odd, and Longarm said, "If Flora Bell is who I suspect she has to be, I can say from personal experience that she is one cool customer who's not inclined to do anything exciting without a good *motive!*"

Vail asked flat out, "Custis, did you lay that wicked gal?"

Longarm sheepishly replied, "I didn't know for certain she was wicked, and *her* motive might have been at least partly recreational. I'm more interested in why she seems to have ordered me killed afterwards. I doubt she's that worried about her reputation. So she or some other mastermind is still worried about me getting warm . . . to what? What are you sending me out on now, if we're shoving all that skullduggery up Canada way and points south to the back of the stove?"

Vail said, "Nothing. It's almost quitting time and they'd finished that Land Management survey we took you off of. I had Deputy Edwards ride herd on those dudes up by Shadow Mountain. Nothing bad happened to any of them, unless you count losing some bacon from the pan to camp-robbing jaybirds. Why don't you run along for now and I'll see if I can find some wood for you to split come morning."

So Longarm got out of there before Vail could change his mind, and seeing it was early for supper, he went over to the Larimer Street Arcade to ask a gent who sold condoms and such if they had that set of French postcards featuring three nuns.

They did. There were seven cards all told, and they were bound in a booklet under the title *Three Young Nuns from Canada,* by the author of the famous *Three Old Maids from Canada*, a Mr. A. Nominus. The words to the poetic captions on the back of each card were much the same, beginning, "Three young nuns from Canada were drinking cherry wine. The song that they were singing was, your hole's no bigger than mine!"

But none of the three gals dressed like nuns, or partly

dressed like nuns, in the seven shocking sepia-tones were wearing any rings at all. Worse yet, none of them looked like Flora Bell or Celine Frazer-Quinn née DuPrix. So *there* went a grand notion. If the one who seemed to be taking the lead with bottles and other tools of the trade was Sister Simone, Longarm had yet to lay eyes on the dirty-grinning gal. So he ambled on up the long gentle slope of Capitol Hill to see if he'd get invited to supper at a certain address on Sherman Street.

The rich young widow woman who received him in her own parlor, all dressed up to go somewhere, seemed delighted to see him, said she'd be proud to feed him, and that then he could escort her to the Adonis Playhouse in time for a new presentation of Mr. Shakespeare's *Much Ado About Nothing.*

He knew better to say he'd seen the fool play and found its title the only thing about it that made sense. His voluptuous hostess with the light brown hair and a bustle that swung like a saloon door on payday served swell suppers and screwed like a mink in heat. So a man had to put up with some of her more annoying habits.

Being a rich widow, she had her own box at the play-house, and he was just as glad. Reporter Crawford from the *Denver Post* was seated in the orchestra row down below, and Longarm had his reasons for not appearing on the social pages. One of them was Miss Morgana Floyd, head matron of the Arvada Orphan Asylum, and there were a couple of other Denver gals who read the society columns as well.

The infernal play started at eight, just as they'd warned everyone. Having sat through the same fool comedy before, Longarm didn't try to follow the chatter on stage that evening. Folks had sure talked odd back in Mr. Shakespeare's time, and a lot of the jokes were either too stale to be funny or too Elizabethan for a Colorado rider to get. As Longarm let his eyes wander about the dimly lit playhouse, his eyes met up with those of another bored-looking gent in the box across the way. They both nodded, each knowing just what the other was thinking as they sweated out *Much Ado About Nothing* with the gussied-up ladies they'd escorted to the fool prancing and preaching contest.

The widow woman Longarm was with nudged him sharply and hissed, "What are you doing, trying to humiliate me? Don't you know who that is across the way?"

Longarm murmured, "Sure I do. We met up in the Wind River country a few summers back. He was hunting buffalo with old Bill Cody. Just for sport. He didn't need the hides. Him and Bill Cody had a contest going as to who could down the most buffalo. Cody let him win, seeing he was paying to be shown a good time in the Wild West. I understand he liked our Wild West so much he decided to stay."

The heiress to a western mining empire replied in a tone of pure venom, "That's for certain! The low-down English upstart has been grabbing land up around Estes Park that was meant to be settled by real Americans, not foreign interlopers!"

Longarm shrugged and said, "I didn't know you and your friends had Indian blood. Estes Park was taken from them pure American Utes by pure American Arapaho, who lost it in turn to Land Management. Estes Park ain't what folks back East call a park, and nobody named Estes has lived there for some time. It was still a grassy mountain vale, or a park in local lingo, grazed by Arapaho ponies, when a Joel Estes and his family horned in, followed by a bunch of MacGregors, I think. The Estes moved on years ago. The MacGregors still graze a good-sized herd up around Estes Park."

"*Around* but hardly *in* all that prime grazing land that English land pirate has helped himself to!" she blazed.

Longarm glanced across at the innocent but bored-looking gent in that other box and replied, "I think he's Irish. I know he's the earl of a heap of Irish farmland.

He was telling us about it, up to the Wind River country, one night after the day's hunt. Said the hunting back in Ireland was nothing next to out our way, and that's likely why he bought that spread up to Estes Park. I never heard anything about him pirating it. I understood he bought it fair and square off homesteaders as may have pirated it from Indians. It was all a spell back."

She firmly stated, "Custis, that unwelcome Earl of Dunraven has not been accepted by Denver Society and during the intermission, I don't want you even nodding at the land-grabbing snob! I mean, who does he think he is, swaggering about Colorado with his fancy English titles and coats of arms on his coach, lording it over everybody while he develops all that alpine scenery he stole from Land Management with new roads, a fancy resort hotel, and all up yonder!"

"How much land did that Earl of Dunraven steal and how did he manage to steal it?" Longarm asked.

She shrugged her shapely shoulders and answered, "How should I know? When my poor husband was alive he tended to such things as mining claims, grazing rights, and land titles. But I have it on the good authority of my own lawyers that your nasty hunting companion, the Earl of Dunraven, pulled a lulu of a land grab up around Estes Park. He's developed his own resort town on close to thirty square miles of his own private estate!"

Longarm whistled softly and allowed he wouldn't drag her over to chat with the wicked Earl of Dunraven, if ever those fool actors on the stage shut up about all that Nothing.

They finally did, and he got to take her home, enjoy some late eggs over chili con carne with her, and take the coffee and cake up to her bedchamber to enjoy dessert in a reclining position.

It sure beat all how different women could be from one another without any of them having to be ugly. She said she'd missed him too, and asked if he'd escort her to a Sunday-Go-to-Meeting-on-the-Green out by the Red Rocks. He answered truthfully that he didn't know what old Billy Vail had in mind for him next. He said, "I like to finish a mission when I'm sent on one, and this last one's left me all proddy and half satisfied. Like having to leave a book half read or never finding out who wound up with a gal who sat next to you in school."

"Was she pretty?" asked an older belle in later times and faraway places he'd never dreamed of when they'd invited him to that war and he'd lost track of things back in West-by-God-Virginia.

He kissed her, told her it was such mysteries that nagged from the cobwebbed corners of his mind, and then they made love for a spell and forgot anybody else had ever dwelt in the same universe.

Later, sharing a smoke with her unbound brown hair spread across his bare chest, she purred, "That was lovely, Custis. Am I forgiven for making you escort me to that comedy by Shakespeare?"

He patted her bare flank and replied, "I like his tragedies better. I couldn't make heads nor tails out of half the jokes in that play this evening. But a good sad story stays as sad and makes as much sense as long as the lingo stays half the same. I enjoyed all them sword fights the time I took you to see *Hamlet*, albeit to tell the pure truth, old Hamlet hisself made me want to kick him as he moped about talking to himself and being mean to that poor Miss Ophelia."

She toyed with his belly hair as she mused, "I might have expected you to root for the ingenue. That's what they call the prettiest girl in a play, dear, the ingenue."

Longarm snorted, "Shoot, I knew what Miss Ophelia was. It was the way Prince Hamlet treated her that made me feel sorry for her. She *liked* him and he had no call to drive her *loco en la cabeza* to where she throwed herself in the river and drowned."

The somewhat more level-headed ingenue of the evening suggested Hamlet had to be mean to his true love so that everyone would think *he* was mad.

Longarm said, "I got that part. Had I been Prince Hamlet and my uncle had murdered my father and got in bed with my mother, I'd have just *killed* the mean rascal. I wouldn't have spent all them acts asking myself if I wanted to be or not to be and ordering poor little Ophelia to get herself to . . . Now that's sort of odd, and I wonder if that's what brought that play about Hamlet to mind tonight. There's these head-examiners over to Vienna Town who say things like that happen when we've been letting our brains chase their tails around."

She demanded, "Custis, whatever are you talking about?"

He said, "That part in the play where Miss Ophelia has Hamlet's head in her lap and they've started to talk sweet, and then he suddenly rears up and yells at her to go join a Papist convent!"

His more formally educated hostess gently pointed out, "Hamlet's exact words, as I recall, were, 'Get thee to a nunnery.' Shakespeare was an Elizabethan Protestant, writing for an audience of his times."

Longarm said, "Crown Sergeant Foster already told me they called a convent a nunnery when he rowed for Harrow. You sure get to admire our own Bill of Rights when you see how some carry on in other places. Up until 1836 no Roman Catholic was allowed to buy land or hold any public office under the British Crown. When an Irishman died with a Catholic son and a Protestant son, the Protestant son got the estate no matter how the will might read."

As the playgoing widow stroked his old organ-grinder to attention, Longarm went on. "Queen Victoria, to her credit, has restored civil rights to her Papist subjects. But they were far down the totem pole under Mr. Shakespeare's Queen Elizabeth, so Mr. Hamlet was low-rating a Danish Protestant lady when he told Miss Ophelia to

167

get her passionate self to a nunnery, right?"

The more formally educated passionate widow forked a shapely bare thigh across Longarm and purred, "My Lord, you have so much to learn, my poor but honest young puncher. But teaching you can be such fun and so, as you say, Powder River and let her buck!"

Chapter 20

Longarm always got an early morning start when he stayed at that particular address. She thought none of her neighbors would know about them if he left by the back gate before dawn. He knew it would have upset her to hear that Billy Vail's wife, down Sherman Street a ways, had been pestering her man about his senior deputy's scandalous affair with that frisky young widow woman, for land's sake.

He took his time and ordered an extra plate of flapjacks with his breakfast. He wanted to be sure of himself before he wired Fort MacLeod. So he waited until the Land Management office was open, and took his time going over a whole lot of ledgers before he decided he was on to something.

It sure beat all how sore some old-timers could get when somebody came along to slicker Indians and Uncle Sam smarter than they had.

The Earl of Dunraven hadn't done anything against statute law. He'd just found a loophole allowing him to grab about thirty square miles of mighty pretty scenery at a price he could afford.

A famous landscape artist named Bierstadt had painted promotional pictures of the earl's Estes Park resort, and helped him design a fine hotel up yonder where dudes from all over could sit in rocking chairs on the veranda and stare at all that swell scenery.

Seeing there was no way to arrest the Earl of Dunraven just for honest greed, Longarm tended to a few other chores around the Federal Building before he headed out to Boulder with Billy Vail's blessings.

He got there just after noon, ambled over to the rental offices of the Elliot estate at Broadway and Pearl, and went upstairs to tell the clerk, Nora, he had a federal search warrant if her boss lady wanted to make a federal case out of it. The scared-looking young gal said she just worked there, and hadn't done a thing but file incoming mail since Mr. Frazer had left her there at her desk on her own. Miss Flora hadn't hired another rental agent as yet.

Longarm smiled down at the bewildered little thing, and suggested she go clear things with her boss lady if she had a mind to. She said she didn't want to leave the office door unlocked with nobody there in charge.

Longarm told her, "I'm in charge till you get back. It may take me some time to go through all the files, seeing I ain't sure just what I'm looking for, see?"

She hesitated, then told him she was holding him accountable if he let anybody steal her typewriting machine.

After she'd left, Longarm had plenty of time to explore the office suite. Like many such business layouts, and every lawyer's office he'd ever been to, the maze of inteconnected rooms had a back way in or out and a whole lot of doors you could shut and bar from either side. Lawyers, and apparently Elliot Enterprises, liked to be set up to play bedroom farces with all sorts of clients slipping in and out of different rooms in the nick of time.

Longarm had picked the late Tom Frazer or Martin Quinn's corner office to settle down in with some real estate plats and a smoke by the time the hefty Flora Bell

170

breezed in with that snooty butler and a tall hungry cuss in a summer-weight suit the color of coal ashes. As Longarm rose to greet her, Flora came around the side of the desk to throw her arms around him and plant a good kiss on his lips before she stepped back to demand in a less friendly tone, "Custis, what's all this I hear about you going through our files without even telling us you were back in town?"

Longarm patted the empty holster at his side, and stared past her at the butler as he calmly replied, "I figured you'd know I was here soon enough, Miss Flora. How come your butler just now grabbed my gun?"

Flora replied in an imperious tone he'd never heard her use on *him* before, "I'll ask the questions here. Before you get the idea you can embarrass me in front of these gentlemen, they both know you've fucked me. I told them I was going to let you before I let you."

Longarm smiled pleasantly and said, "The one as has my gun opened the door for me up at your place. This other gent has the advantage on me."

The gray suit said, "Let's just say I'm Madam's lawyer. What's this shit about you having a search warrant?"

Longarm said, "I lied. I asked Judge Dickerson down in Denver for a search warrant, and he said I'd failed to show just cause. I didn't have enough to justify going over your books. Judge Dickerson can be such a fuss about rules of evidence. Would you like to call the law on me for trespassing up here without permission?"

Flora Bell laughed, not a pretty sound, and said, "That'll be the day! We don't need any other lawmen up here today, handsome. Nate here carries a private investigator's license as well as a .455. Before I have you shot as a common thief caught in the act, why don't you tell us what on earth you were looking for up here?"

Longarm asked with sincere interest if Nate's license as well as his service revolver were British-issue.

The suddenly less feminine Flora snapped, "Never

mind all that. It won't do you any good to stall, Custis. We scouted around downstairs before we came up to have it out with you. There's nobody here but us chickens, and I know for a fact there's not one shred of incriminating evidence in Martin's files. There never *was* a shred of incriminating evidence in any files. What sort of chumps do you take us for?"

Longarm easily replied, "Land-grabbing chumps. I say chumps because the way the Earl of Dunraven did it was a little more expensive but way easier on the nerves. I've been going over Colorado land claims down at the Land Management office in Denver. His and yours, or those of the late Red Jim Elliot."

She snapped, "Don't get cute with us. Red Jim didn't leave any paper trails for you Yankee federal snoops. Every land title held by Elliot Enterprises is held free and clear with ironbound deeds that will stand up in any court!"

Longarm said, "I noticed. You should have quit while you were ahead, Miss Flora. Red Jim might have known how to swing it. I'm sure the two of you talked about what the Earl of Dunraven was doing as you were going dog-style up in that tower bed."

"Kill him," Flora Bell commanded.

But the gray suit called Nate shook his head and said, "Not yet. I want to hear now if there was any point to this conversation, lest I wind up losing sleep about it later."

He casually raised the Webley Bulldog he'd been holding down at his side as he calmly added, "Get to the point, Yank. You know you've already gone too far. But we can make it as easy or as hard as you ask for it."

The occasional butler had his own six-gun out by now, leaving only Flora and Longarm unarmed as Longarm sighed and said, "What the Earl of Dunraven was doing, over in Estes Park just a spit and a holler from here, was unscrupulous but perfectly legal under the provisions of the Homestead Act of '63. Being a foreigner, the earl was allowed to *buy* land free and simple from American citizens. The Queen of England owns a big chunk of New York City she collects rent on from Irish tenants who'd have a fit if they knew. But neither she nor any of her earls would be allowed to file on a hundred and sixty acres under the Homestead Act. So the earl hired a whole army of poor but honest American citizens to file adjoining claims over in Estes Park. Four families to the square mile. About a hundred such nesters all told. He backed their play with the cash it took to file and prove their claims. Once they had, five years after he'd put the whole plot together, the earl simply bought all hundred or so adjoining homesteads and wrapped his bob wire around the whole estate. Some other land speculators who hadn't thought of that first are still mad at him. But nobody got hurt."

Flora Bell quietly insisted, "Kill him. He doesn't know *merde*!"

The gray suit told Longarm to keep talking.

Longarm said, "As Red Jim, or mayhaps the lady here, noticed, the Earl of Dunraven would have wound up with an even bigger private spread up in the mountains had all his hired homesteaders played fair. But there's always someone who gets greedy and spoils it for everybody. So by the time the earl had amassed his first twenty or thirty square miles, some of the homesteaders he'd backed held out for more money than they'd agreed on. They figured they had him over a barrel. They figured him wrong. Unlike some I could mention, the Earl of Dunraven could push away from the table after he'd had enough. So he told them to just keep their scenery, and by the way, pay back the notes he held on their grubstakes, and that was the end of the party up around Estes Park. Others moved in to buy up grazing rights or scenery, and Red Jim must have felt a tad left out."

The dirty old man's plump play-pretty sneered, "I told

you he knows nothing! Elliot Enterprises owns not one square foot west of the Flatirons yet."

Longarm said, "*Yet* is the magic word. Red Jim had grabbed the easy pickings here in Boulder County. When he heard them Indian lands west of here were about to be thrown open to homesteading, Red Jim commenced the planning you sweet kids bungled, trying to carry on. Red Jim and likely all you earlier Canadian real-estate mongers had been here long enough to apply for citizenship. But you could only apply for a hundred and sixty acres of mountain scenery at a time. So you sent away for outside help, knowing that no Canadian outlaw posing as an American citizen with a name as sweet could double-cross you."

He shook his head wearily and asked, "Were you planning to pay them off as promised or as you paid off Constable LeClerc? The plan was for him to get sort of lost in the mountains, right?"

Nate said, "You're right. You're dead. But before we say *adieu,* who told you so much, that species of *petite bête* Celine?"

Longarm said, "She keeps telling us she wasn't in on the whole plan. You gave the game away when you offered me a seat at the table. *We* thought the Mounties had asked for me by name, and *they* thought I'd been volunteered by the U.S. Justice Department, after somebody sent a few slick wires. You can sign any name in dots and dashes."

The one posing as a butler sort of sobbed, "*Merde alors!* I warned you not to be so clever, and now look at the *souffle* we must deflate!"

The one in the gray suit replied defensively, "It was worth a try. He knew that recent Indian country better than those government survey men could have. You see how fast he thinks on his feet!"

Longarm said, "I might have never noticed those so-called trappers camped casual all about Shadow Mountain had you kept their numbers more modest, and your other moves were too cute from the first, had you been working with a more disciplined gang. You should have seen it wasn't going to work when some of them took to murder and highway robbery on their own. But you thought you'd deflected that attention from the law up Fort Collins way, and when you heard I was riding herd on the dudes surveying land you wanted to grab, you tried to deflect *me* up to Fort Collins as well. How many times did Sister Simone and her fake Canadian lawman, Chambrun-Masterson, have to drive back and forth across an unmarked wild border before those part-time deputies paid a lick of attention to them?"

The formidable Flora sighed. "I'm sorry you were as quick on the trigger as Red Jim warned, Custis. It was more fun to just try and fool you. I suppose that prissy little snip Celine told you all about our *tres amusante* Sister Simone, *hein*?"

Longarm said, "I told you she's either loyal or ignorant, ma'am. It was Mr. Will Shakespeare as told me where to arrest Sister Simone, if ever I get out of here alive."

Flora made a wry face and said, "You won't. What are we to do with this loose cannon, Nate?"

The gray suit said, "Put your hands behind you, loose cannon."

Longarm smiled thinly and said, "I was wondering how you got Tom Frazer or Martin Quinn to let you do this to him up to Cheyenne. But before this party gets any rougher, have any of you ever been to that play *Hamlet, Prince of Denmark* by Mr. William Shakespeare?"

The three of them exchanged bewildered glances. Flora Bell said, "Of course we have! Do you take us for uneducated clods like you?"

Longarm went on smiling as he said, "I noticed what refined manners you had, Miss Flora. In that play, as you may recall, Hamlet is jawing with his mother in her

175

chambers when he notices Miss Ophelia's daddy hiding behind some hanging drapes. He doesn't know who it is listening in. He thinks it's his wicked uncle, the king, so the next thing you know he's whupped out his dagger and stabbed the nosy Mr. Polonius with his dirk through the drapes. It's a real tragic scene as leaves an impression on you."

The one called Nate demanded, "What in the hell are you talking about? What does a play by Shakespeare have to do with whether you put your damned hands behind your damned back or not?"

Longarm said, "I borrowed the notion from Mr. Shakespeare, with the difference that I *knew* who was hiding behind the drapes, or in this case, doors. So I reckon that's our cue to enter stage right and left!"

At which point doors popped open from two sides and all hell broke loose.

Longarm dropped to one knee as Nate fired through the space he'd just been in. As he raised the double derringer palmed in his big fist, Deputy Smiley from the Denver office shot Nate to make a bloody mess on the corner of Broadway and Pearl by spinning him out the window, glass and all. So Longarm shot the butler instead as the latter fired wild.

Then things got quiet enough for the shorter deputy they called Dutch to stare out the far door through the smoke with his own .44–40 unfired, muttering, "Aw, heck, some jaspers have all the fun!"

Flora Bell was against the far wall, leaning against a filing cabinet as she stared wide-eyed at Longarm.

His tone was fair but firm as he told her, "It's over, Miss Flora. You might still save your neck with a full confession, though."

She softly replied, *"Mais non! C'est une petite faute!"*

Then she slid down the wall to her knees and pitched forward to land face-down, limp as a bear rug.

Deputy Smiley stared soberly at the long red streak

176

she'd left on the wall, and said, "It wasn't me. Did you understand what she was saying just now, pard?"

Longarm decided, "I think she was trying to tell us it was all a mistake. I don't see as her exact words matter now."

Chapter 21

Crown Sergeant Foster of the Royal Canadian Mounted Police had been busy as a one-armed paperhanger in a windstorm. So he'd wired back for some time off, and it was nearly a week later when he was sharing the free lunch in a Boulder saloon on the seedy side of the over-sized UC campus, along with some of that popular lager brewed down the Front Range. He was looking more comfortable in his scarlet and gold.

As he washed down some pickled pigs-feet, Foster asked in a jovial tone what Longarm and his fellow Yanks had done to inspire such a vast migration of outlaws wanted by the Crown.

Foster went on. "Thanks to your earlier warning wires, and my recognizing that one wanted in Cheyenne, we cracked the murder of Frazer-Quinn when he rode into our reinforced border patrols and it became a matter of *chacun a son gout*!"

When Longarm looked blank, the French-speaking Mountie translated, "Every man for himself. There's no honor among thieves, and having heard their leaders have all been killed . . ."

Foster stared wistfully and sighed. "I wish I could have

been there. Sounds like the last act of *Hamlet,* complete with the death of Queen Gertrude!"

Longarm said, "We figure the butler did it. It was just as well. When I got back to Denver to hand in my report, I caught pure Ned from our legal eagles. They held I had no constitutional right to set up that trap on private property without a real writ from Judge Dickerson. But I knew he'd never give me one on the evidence I had. So I invited my pals Smiley and Dutch to tag along informal. I had them wait out front while I spooked that clerk gal out of the office, and after that it was simple to let my pals in and hide 'em out within earshot. The rest you know, if you read that night letter I wired Fort MacLeod at off-hour rates."

Foster chuckled fondly and said, "Your more polished legal staff in Denver was right. You didn't have enough solid evidence for a conviction if they'd stood their ground instead of running in on you with their fangs bared. Whatever possessed you to take such a chance, Long? Even with your backup riders listening in, you could have wound up very dead by taunting cold-blooded killers like that!"

Longarm shrugged and said, "You do what you have to, and like we've all agreed, I needed more than an educated guess. I'd have never seen the pattern at all if they hadn't been too clever by half for their own good. Had they left me be, showing Land Management dudes how to back a tick out of your hide without busting its head off under the skin, I might or might not have noticed them anxious squatters set up around Shadow Mountain to rush in and stake out quarter sections the moment we finished the survey and departed. If they hadn't ordered their famously sinful Sister Simone to stage that border incident and plant that stolen watch in Fort Collins, the two of us might have wound up scouting farther from here. They had no control over Celine Frazer-Quinn blowing holes in Constable LeClerc right in town after they'd lured him down this way to bury him somewhere more discreet. But they should have known better than to drag her away from her own housekeeping chores and into a game too rough for her."

He helped himself to a deviled egg and continued. "I was talking to her this morning, over to the county jail, and I'll be switched with snakes if I don't expect her to get off. Her man—Martin, as she recalls him—was in on the land-grabbing plans up to his eyebrows. But he really hadn't told her much, and neither expected the horny LeClerc to take her for as rough and ready a slut as the Sister Simone he'd already had three ways for the asking."

Foster glanced about and declared, "You told me in your last wire that your superior, Marshal Vail, wanted to offer Sister Simone to Crown Justice with no strings?"

Longarm washed down the deviled egg, reached for a wedge of cheese, and replied, "On a silver platter. Two reasons. Most of the sins she's wanted for, including that set of French postcards, took place up Canada way. So she's a British subject who never committed a federal crime on U.S. soil, as far as we can prove."

Foster frowned thoughtfully and decided, "I can see she seduced Constable LeClerc in Canmont, and then he was killed by somebody else here in Colorado. But what about that charade in that Fort Collins pawnshop?"

Longarm replied, "What about it? Hocking a watch stolen in another country constitutes a local investigation, and likely a stern warning from a local judge as long as she said she'd been given said watch for a blow job in an alley and had no idea where it might have come from. We don't think she was mixed up in the highway robbery and murder of that silver-spurred Gus Persson earlier. If she was in these parts at all that far back, highway robbery ain't her style. She's a wanton show-off and troublemaker who inspires others to raise hell. She don't work so good as an out-and-out road agent."

Foster stiffly remarked, "We'll let Her Majesty's Canadian judge and jury decide that. You said there were *two* reasons?"

Longarm grabbed for some salami as he nodded and explained. "Like you said, chase-a-young-goat when it comes to doing time for others wanted by the law. Once Mr. Will Shakespeare put me on to Sister Simone's likely hideout, I just had to show those naughty pictures of her to a handful of shady folks with no visible means of support until I found one as knew her and, better yet, had her current address. It had to be somewhere in these parts if she was working with a local gang of shady Canadians."

Foster said, "That's right! She was the one who lured that innocent dupe, Jacques Cartier or Jack Carter, to that fatal poker game and then she helped them frame him by . . . Oh, I say!"

"She never did," Longarm told him, washing down some salami before he went on. "It sure beats all how tough it can be to find a convicted felon willing to admit he done the deed. When they ain't jacking off in their cells, they're making up more excuses for themselves, and Jack Carter's tale was plausible, up to a point. He'd been in on that unauthorized robbery with other restless young riders from up your way. So he knew all about the Flatiron Hotel being a way station, and Sister Simone was likely the one who'd shown it to him when he first rode down from the High Plains of Canada. So he tried to sell the state of Colorado a yarn about an innocent lamb led astray. The lying son of a bitch."

"How can you be so sure?" asked the other lawman, who knew the same sad story.

Longarm said, "It only sounds good the first time you take it in. When you go back over it, trying to picture things step by step, it steps in some holes."

He tried another deviled egg as he explained. "Carter-Cartier said he'd been working his way up the Front

181

Range in roundup time, looking in vain for work. That's about the only time I know when a wandering saddle tramp can pick up some easy day wages. There's never enough help on hand during roundup time, when all the spreads join in to gather in the free-ranging stock for cutting into separate herds. So let's say nobody he asked along the way liked the cut of his jib, and let's say Sister Simone picked up another Canadian by pure accident off a campus bench so she could lure him into that card game at a hideout they didn't want others to know about, to frame him for a killing he might have had an ironclad alibi for, seeing he'd just shown up in their neck of the woods."

Foster nodded and said, "I was wondering more about that train ride up to Fort Collins."

Longarm swallowed and said, "It's three stops, even when you ain't spending two days in the saddle. But let's say you *could* keep a stranger in these parts too drunk to know where he was until you could ditch him in Fort Collins and have him picked up for a crime he didn't know a thing about. He'd have surely sobered up by the time he even saw his appointed defense, and no matter how much two towns resemble one another, and Boulder and Collins are laid out different, how stupid would any man have to be to act *that* stupid, and even if they thought he was, it was too big a boo for such sneaks to take. They had no way of knowing who a total stranger might have met up with earlier in Boulder. They had no way of knowing a wandering rider had never passed through such a nearby town as Collins before. In sum, they didn't hang the wrong man. The lying shit pawned them spurs in Collins and got caught. His pals gunned that pawnbroker for catching him. Flora Bell and the other ringleaders had nothing to do with it. So neither did Sister Simone, a mere maid-of-all-work to Miss Flora, and no doubt a bit of occasional fun for the boys."

Crown Sergeant Foster declared, "You've convinced

me, and I can't wait to slap the cuffs on her. But where on earth have you been hiding her? There isn't any RC nunnery this side of Denver. We're not going down to Denver from here, are we?"

Longarm said, "I'd be proud to show you around down yonder if you want to ask Boulder County to hold her for you a few days. But we only have to walk downwind another few streets, Sarge. They ought to be open for early arrivals any time now. Some of these rich college kids ought to be ashamed of themselves, cutting classes to get laid on the money sent from home for books and such."

"You're taking me to a *whorehouse*?" the Mountie asked with a puzzled smile.

Longarm finished the last of his suds, belched, and explained, "That's what Sister Simone is. A low-down show-off slut who rents her various body orifices by the hour cheap. She and two other whores posed for them French postcards in a studio made up to look like it was a convent cell. A more serious Papist barmaid put me on to their lack of proper jewelry. My pal, Sergeant Nolan of the Denver police, told me that one nun with ear bobs and French heels on her high-buttons looked all wrong too, once he got over his shock. They were posed in those religious costumes to add to the shock. You expect a *whore* to shove a wine bottle up her twat or rub titties with another whore, but when it looks like two nuns in a convent acting so dirty, it seems way more dirty. I understand the same trio posed for another set of poses with a mighty friendly bloodhound. But I've yet to see that one. It sounds sort of disgusting. Finish your beer and let's get cracking."

Foster did, and they left to make Foster's arrest for the Crown.

Along the way, Foster glanced about at the increasingly run-down housing and weedy yards and remarked, "It's no wonder the Archbishop of Montreal seemed so insulted when we asked which nunnery the notorious Sister Simone might be hiding in between rampages!"

Longarm said, "We grow our own self-styled legends down our way. Like Deadwood Dick, Calamity Jane, and even Buffalo Bill, to hear some tell it. Wandering frontier characters with tricky nicknames don't have to lie that much themselves to become larger than life. As a whore inclined to put on dirty shows in a nun's wimple and rosary beads, your Simone Blanchard, as she was sprinkled by a Church she's turned her back on, got better known as a notorious renegade nun as she traipsed your Canadian West, screwing everything from any Cree in town with the money to rich tourists anxious to experience the Wild West. When things got hot for her, she'd hole up as a regular whore and wait for things to cool off. Since she'd been mixed up in serious robberies up your way, she's been spending most of her time here in Boulder at the establishment of a Madam DePrave. I suspect that may be what some call a name changed for business reasons. Madam DePrave has made a deal through our mutual pal, Sergeant Nolan of the Denver police, who vacations up this way on occasion. It was another Denver lowlife who told me he'd seen Sister Simone put on a show for the college boys up this way. They say grown men come from all around when Sister Simone gets really dirty."

Foster said, "Look out for that dead cat on the path ahead. This is getting dirty indeed. But didn't that Jewess up in Fort Collins overhear Sister Simone telling her chum in the derby hat she was heading home to her nunnery?"

Longarm nodded and said, "Mr. Will Shakespeare had a low opinion of her former faith as well. Most folks today miss his meaning when he has Hamlet tell the poor lovesick Miss Ophelia to go join up at a nunnery. To us it sounds as if Hamlet's advising her to forget about fornication as a Papist nun. But he's really telling her to run off to play with other whores and leave him the hell alone."

Foster frowned and said, "I say, that does sound like an awfully rude thing to say to a girl who's in love with you. It's no wonder she runs offstage weeping. But I distinctly recall the line and it does read, *Get thee to a nunnery*!"

Longarm nodded soberly and said, "Queen Elizabeth's dad, Henry VIII, went to feud with the Pope in Rome and grabbed all Church property in England, even though he liked that title the Pope had given him as a Defender of the Faith and held on to it. By the time Hamlet was writ, all the *real* nunneries in England had been shut down for years. So the term had been transferred sarcastically to the whorehouses of Mr. Will Shakespeare's day. His audiences must have snickered more when Hamlet told that poor Danish Protestant lady of quality to get her pretty self to a nunnery. The gal as explained all this to me says Shakespeare's plays are full of dirty double meanings. That might be why educated folks enjoy him more. Did you know that when Hamlet asks Miss Ophelia if she's come to talk about country matters, he's using another sneaky double meaning his London audiences would have used? When you say it as it's pronounced, country matters can be taken as *cuntry* matters."

He pointed at a barn-red three-story frame across the next unpaved north-south street and said, "Yonder's the nunnery Sister Simone has been running home to for the last few summers. What say you work your way about to the back, while I give you the time it takes to finish a cheroot, and we'll see if I can flush her towards you."

So that was how they worked it. Crown Sergeant Foster strode into an alleyway leading behind the barn-red nunnery, and hunkered behind a compost pile out back while Longarm strode up the front steps to pound importantly on the door with his pocket derringer and bellow, "Open in the name of the law, lest I huff, and puff, and blow your house in!"

So a few minutes later Foster came around the side of the house holding a kicking and spitting Simone Blanchard by the links between her handcuffs as the swarthy and disappointingly drab Métis pleaded with the triumphant Mountie to let her have her shoes and unmentionable undergarments before they took her home to hang.

So the firm but fair Foster took her upstairs for her unmentionables, while Longarm had a drink at the bar with the raddled Madam DePrave.

Thus, a little over forty-eight hours later, Longarm was seated in Billy Vail's inner office as the portly marshal went over the final report Henry had typed up for him out front.

Vail finally decided, "You did all right, considering. But if you saw that Mountie off with his prisoner two full days ago, where have you been ever since?"

Longarm flicked some tobacco ash on the floor to discourage carpet mites and explained, "Had some things to tidy up when the case ended sort of messy. I felt responsible for this poor little clerk gal, seeing I'd sort of cost her a good job. So I stayed up yonder a spell to help her get another. She's working for the county now, as happy as all get-out."

Vail cocked a brow to growl, "So much for the last two *days*. What about the last two *nights*?"

Longarm calmly replied, "I'm going to pretend I never heard that question, and since there are some questions no gentleman ever asks or answers, I reckon we'll just never know, will we?"